"Gentlemen, from the day the land first rose from the sea, giants have walked the earth. They raged in the wake of the first thunderstorms, ripping apart the primeval forests. Masters of the land before men lived there, they seemed enraged at the intrusion of fragile creatures of flesh.

"And still they strike at random, without warning, at any hour of the day or night. They leave behind them smashed homes, broken lives, the mutilated dead. In the paths of these old blind furies, strong men are as helpless and fearful as children. The awesome strength of tornadoes has always been accepted as unchallengeable.

"Until now. Gentlemen, you hold in your hands the power to *end* the terror of

Tornado Alley

Tornado Alley

By

WILLIAM TUNING

SF
ace books

A Division of Charter Communications Inc.
A GROSSET & DUNLAP COMPANY
360 Park Avenue South
New York, New York 10010

TORNADO ALLEY

An ACE Book

Cover art by David Schleinkoffer

First Ace printing: December 1978

Printed in U.S.A.

Chapter 1

It was not a drill.

The warning klaxon and scramble bell fell into an urgent cadence, counterpointed by human feet running across the concrete apron. Three white-clad figures leaped from the jolly-wagon, and sprinted toward the garishly lighted flight-line.

0305 hours. The stars seem to hang at treetop level in the moonless rainwashed sky.

Three needle-nosed, stub-wing aircraft squatted with turbines already turning. As each pilot buckled in, the canopy locked shut. "System go" lights flashed at the mission control console: the launch signal passed to the watch commander. The computer system paused, waiting for the human link.

Fingers darted over the boards. The watch commander pressed the "go" button.

The concrete apron shook under the impact of bellowing afterburners. Three slender craft leaped into the air like quarrels from a giant crossbow, accelerating up a seventy-degree incline.

Within ninety seconds, they leveled out forty-five thousand feet above Topeka, Kansas, on a northeast heading. Jill-Leader accelerated to Mach 2.5. She would reach the target in twelve minutes, followed at one-minute intervals by Jill-Two and Jill-Three.

Soon they were whistling over a deepening layer of ragged, swirling clouds. Each carried a five-ton egg in her belly. Fertilized under precisely controlled conditions this egg could hatch into a giant-killer. At the proper instant it would blossom into a white-hot globe of flame over two hundred meters in diameter.

Nine minutes after launch Jill Flight was over three hundred miles away.

"Jill-Leader to Topeka. Confirm readouts."

"This is Topeka Jill-Leader. I have you bearing seven-four. Straight in at three-six."

"Roger Topeka. That's a positive confirm. I have target *on* screen."

"Ah, roger. Jill-Leader. Topeka copies target acquired. Go in and stop him, kid. Target plot-out and CompAn update has him coming toward Palmyra. ETA six minutes. Moving at eighteen knots. Come to heading six-niner."

"Roger, Topeka. Jill-Leader copy new heading of zero-six-niner. Coming up on IP. Confirm on bomb-run. IPO now *on* computer and ready for attack. Break voice transmission. Ready to mark on IP"

Mountainous thunderheads billowed beneath Jill Flight, though the enemy drew life from a disturbance over Hannibal, Missouri. Lightning ripped livid seams in the churning air below. From two miles above, where Jill-Leader began her bomb-run, the flashes appeared as faint orange flashes and dull glows winking under the tortured clouds. Otherwise, the night inside the cloud system was as black as a witches' brew on Walpurgis.

Jill-Leader put her nose down, throttled back, and watched the towering enemy grow on the screen. She dropped into the darkness, slowing to subsonic. At this point she was dependent on the "soup-screen" for navigation. The giant, invisible to human eyes in the whirling murk, had picked up speed over open farm land. Now it was walking at twenty-one knots toward Palmyra, a village ten miles above Hannibal. From an IP five miles distant, the final run was straight and level at eighteen hundred feet. Straight and level through air as wild as any typhoon sea.

When the screen reticle centered on the shadowy monster, Jill-Leader switched the autopilot to AT-TACK, and held tight. The gust-battered craft, now moving at a five-hundred knot crawl, pulled up into a programmed arc and laid her egg precisely at the correct instant. The plane accelerated up and through the boiling clouds in a steep Immelman taking her back the way she had come. Behind a five-ton, explosive egg carved toward the distant target.

In the ward room of Jill Flight's base there is a glass wall that affords a clear view of the control center. Behind that glass the Commanding Officer moves restlessly. At the readout console, he punches up monitor sequences that let him read over the controllers' shoulders. He fits his large frame into a straight chair, one long leg up against his chest. Chin on his knee, he studies the light patterns on the electronic situation map, plotting the location and progress of Jill Flight's destruct mission.

This routine will be repeated ceaselessly until the last plane is down. He might break for cigarettes, coffee, or phone calls, but never stops his systematic intake of the mission's rapidly changing information.

This mission isn't like the old days in Nam. There's no flak or enemy aircraft. No missiles stamped "Made in USSR" crouching in the jungle, waiting to grease Yankee pilots. Now, his planes aren't shot at, but aircraft do go down. Pilots did die. He stared for a long time at the corner of the plotting table—without really seeing it.

It was true that female pilots in the U.S. Air Force were no longer any great novelty. Captain Chelsey Quincannon was as sharp as they came. Had he over-stepped a little by putting a woman in the flight leader's spot? He was going to have to rate her for promotion. He wasn't going to please everyone—no matter what he decided.

Such questions haunt a waiting commander. He wonders how his people are doing, without being able to *do* anything himself. He is utterly helpless, his people are on their own. How carefully has he prepared them for the combat? Has he been too loose with them? Has he gone too far the other way and overtrained them? Will they succeed? The most persistent question is what will it cost? Will the price go as high as a human life?

The Commanding Officer stalks around the ward room, drinks coffee, and studies the readouts.

The continent was new. The land came up from the sea and the air moved across it. Clouds grew in the air and cast their shadows. Between land and cloud, the giants walked.

The continent was new. New clouds grew in the air and cast their shadows. Between land and cloud, the giants walked, masters of the earth, destroying everything they touched, unchallengeable.

And so it was, until the time of "Jill the Giant-Killer."

Four-year-old Jill lay sobbing hysterically on a chilly hillside, her face buried in the wet grass. She had been there long enough that the tears no longer came from her eyes, despite the sobs that ripped all the air from her lungs and left her shivering for breath.

That morning, her mother had dressed her in a yellow-gold dress as delicate as a butterfly's wing. The fluffy skirt made her feel nearly weightless as she pirouetted before the big mirror in the hall of her parent's house.

She was going to town with Mother and Daddy. It would be pretty. It was springtime on the prairie. Daddy would get the car and bring it up to the house. She could sit in the back seat and look out the window. Coming back to the farm, later, she would sit in the back seat and be surrounded with the nice smells of the groceries. She would snuggle in among the brown paper bags as though she, too, was a sack of provisions.

Suddenly, the mirror nodded away from the wall and shattered in front of her. The whole world seemed to explode at once. The nice house disappeared and she was on a hillside, cold and miserable. She sat up and looked around, but couldn't see very well. It was raining very hard. She pushed wet hair away from her face. Mother had braided her red hair just a little while ago; tied ribbons in it that matched the dress. Now, it had all come unbraided. The ribbons were gone. Her yellow dress was wet and limp and clung coldly to her.

Jill got to her feet and began to walk through the rain. She wanted to find her mother and daddy. She didn't know how long she walked or where she went. She finally found them, though, where the house had been.

The house was gone. Broken lumber spread in a crazy pattern around the foundation. Jill was frightened. Daddy was in the yard near the driveway. He looked as though he were taking a nap on the grass, except that his face and hands were very white. Jill couldn't get him to wake up. When she found her mother, lying in a way that looked awfully uncomfortable, she sat down very carefully next to her. When it began to get dark, she discovered that Mother wouldn't wake up either.

She was still there when they found her the next morning. After the storm had passed, the Army

National Guard was mobilized to search for sur-
vivors and prevent looting. They marveled that the
twister had so completely destroyed the house and
killed Jill's father and mother without harming her.
No one realized that she had been picked up in the
vortex and dropped on a hillside over a mile away.
No one knew of her trek back to where her home
had once been.

She never told anyone. Terrified and exhausted,
but queasily happy that there *were* other people
alive after all, Jill began to forget as soon as the
guardsmen wrapped her in a warm blanket. She was
fast asleep long before they got her to the disaster
center. It was past. It was something like a bad
dream by the time her grandmother arrived from
California.

She never told anyone. She was alive while her
parents were dead. That was impossible for her to
understand. All that remained of that day was a
recurring nightmare full of incredible noise and
fear.

Chapter 2

Senator Pogue spoke from the chairman's seat at the head of the table. "The committee will now hear the Junior Senator from California," he drawled. "It is our understandin' that she has *remarks* of interest on our budget considerations for Armed Forces appropriations." He smiled rather vacantly as she rose, "Senator Kernan . . ."

The California Senator was a smallish woman with red hair, a Duke of Wellington nose, and a speaking voice that could shatter a beer mug at twenty paces. She was at once a plain talker and a slippery adversary in debate.

"I can understand and am willing to support the proposition"—her green eyes swept the oak-

paneled room—"that a strong defense force is
needed in peacetime. So long as militant
nationalists rule anywhere in the world, anything
less would be stupid. The capability, if not the
naked threat, of nuclear annihilation is the only
language men of that stripe can clearly understand
and respect.

"Our own defense posture, though, must not be
measured by the size of the military *budget* alone.
Chicken colonels, sitting on their duffs reading
each other's memos, do not constitute a strong defense."

Jill looked up and down the table with what she
hoped was an intimidating gaze. Senator Pogue, the
seemingly senile Committee Chairman, sat unblink-
ing. One could never tell if his hearing aid was
working or if he was even alive enough for that to
matter.

She continued. "You gentlemen know as well as
I do that an effective defense force requires vigilance, competence, and challenge. Paper shufflers
aren't vigilant. We need lean, agile fighters, *not* an
army of clerks. A *fighting* force guided by effective
leaders is capable of instant response. But, unim-
aginative and unchallenging war *games* do not produce such a force, or such leaders.

"A constituent of mine—one who is highly re-
garded in the scientific community—has developed
a suggestion of great merit which both serves these
goals and is of immediate material benefit to the
taxpaying electorate. I urge you to give it serious
consideration."

There are different states of awareness in a Senate
committee. There is the awareness of those who

have a serious regard for the public trust of their office. There is also the simple wariness of those coming up for re-election in the fall. Several committee members pricked up their ears at the juxtaposition of merit-defense, and material benefit. These are magic words.

"What he proposes," she said, "is one method of keeping our military in fighting trim and on its toes technologically. He has conceived a peacetime mission for the Air Force that will save some several hundred lives and over a half a billion dollars in property damage *each year*. Right here at home."

Senator Pogue, still staring straight ahead, slowly lifted his right hand, pointing toward the ceiling with his index finger. His expression did not change. Jill Kernan paused, uncertain of the chairman's gesture. His finger crooked as he scratched his ear energetically.

She continued deliberately, "What is proposed is air warfare against a natural enemy. Warfare against a force that has been killing and maiming Americans since the Pilgrims landed."

She leaned forward and spoke with quiet emphasis, "I have been assured that our existing weapons capability is equal to the task of killing tornadoes." She smiled before quickly repeating herself in the second of silence that followed. "Yes, *killing tornadoes*."

There were the expected exclamations and muttering among the committee members. Chairman Pogue's left eye made two tics in rapid succession. She wondered if he had been listening or was just surprised by the commotion.

Jill waved her hand gracefully for quiet. "His

analysis will show—if the committee will hear his study proposals—that a tornado can be broken up by a special kind of bomb, *without* risk to people or structures in the immediate areas.

"We have the tools necessary for the job. Both the Navy and the Air Force have perfected the pitch-bombing maneuver required to deliver the bomb. Both these services have supersonic aircraft capable of reaching the tornado within minutes of the initial spotting. We have an effective nation-wide aircraft/ground communication system in operation. We have the radar net and the computer hardware needed to direct the operation. Proper organization of our available technology can kill tornadoes. Any questions?"

Senator Thurlow cleared his throat noisily, making his jowls quiver. When certain of everyone's attention, he carefully ran his hand through his thick, iron-gray hair. He wore it vaingloriously styled in a longish version of the "elder statesman" cut. It was, with his bushy eyebrows, a large part of his image as a good old boy who had made it in the U.S. Senate.

"*Miss* Kernan, *honey*, are you suggesting the U.S. Air Force be set after chasing twisters around the country like a bunch of Flash Gordons? In *rocket planes?*" He paused to let his cronies chuckle. "Why we'd be the laughingstock of the rest of the world—and then some."

Jill's green eyes narrowed. Senator Thurlow awaited her reply with a look of complete naiveté. He was in his favorite role, the country bumpkin about to skin the slicker. It was a trap Jill knew.

"*Miss* Kernan?" she asked innocently. "*Senator* Kernan—let the record show—suspects from the question that her learned colleague may be afflicted with ossifying intellect. We're seeking *meaningful* spending programs, Senator. Programs that will accomplish preparedness while benefitting the country *right now*."

"Well honey, we all know that," Thurlow soothed. He looked at everyone up and down the table. "That's what we're *here* for, isn't it?" He paused, again, to let his cronies chuckle at his pedestrian instruction of Jill in the obvious. "And, I resent your implications that I am an old fossil. 'Ossifying intellect,' indeed. I shall, if pressed, appeal to the chair for relief from abuse." He smiled good-naturedly, just to show that he was "only funnin'."

At the word "chair," Senator Pogue's eyelids snapped open like window shades. He looked carefully around the table without moving to determine if he was being addressed or only referred to.

"How would you recommend flight officers earn their pay and maintain proficiency?" Jill asked. "Flying luncheon junkets to Miami? Congressional 'fact-finding missions' to international resort spots?"

Jill knew by the mutterings up and down the table that she had tweaked a nerve. She decided to back off on that point. "Gentlemen, the best defensive posture is one in which your fighting force is clearly ready for anything that comes along. What better way to demonstrate readiness than to wage incessant warfare against a *natural* enemy as formidable and destructive as our annual crop of tornadoes? This is one war that can only be applauded by other countries. This would be a war to save lives. The value of property saved from destruction would exceed the cost of the program. Think about *that*." She paused for breath. "Senator Tannenbaum? You wished to comment?"

"Thank you, Senator Kernan, Jake Tannenbaum smiled. "I find myself in full agreement with the goals you have stated, but I *am* a mite skeptical of the feasibility of Dr. Graham's program. Your scientist friend is Vernon Graham—yes?"

Jill nodded, as Tannenbaum continued.

"I think it a good idea," he said, "for Dr. Graham to give us a detailed briefing of the scientific bases on which his proposal rests."

Senator Thurlow grumbled. "That pointy-headed liberal will not be welcome in *this* chamber, Senator. So, this year he longs to tell us how to spend those defense dollars he squalled so loud about our getting *last* year. I reckon he finds nothing wrong with our budget if he can get some of it for his own pet ideas!"

"Wonder of wonders!" exclaimed Jill. "Never thought I'd see the day Senator Thurlow would object to military spending. Are you quite well, sir?"

Above the general laughter, Thurlow responded with a hearty politician's chuckle. "Touché, honey. You've gone and pinked this old fossil in a vital spot." He paused, as if to take the pulse of the committee. "If these gentlemen are agreeable, and our revered colleague, Chairman Pogue, consents, perhaps we can hear this egghead friend of yours at next week's meeting."

"So moved," Jake Tannenbaum said quickly.

"Second," Jill chirped.

Senator Pogue's eyelids snapped open. "Fu'ther debate?"

Silence.

"Favor?" Pogue rasped.

Jumbled assent from the table.

" 'Posed?"

Silence.

"Drawin' close to lunch time," Pogue re-marked.

"Thank you, gentlemen," Jill said. "And,"—she turned to Thurlow— "very gallant of you, sir. I take back my previous unkind implication."

Thurlow bowed graciously.

"You aren't all that old," Jill said.

The stony image at the head of the table slowly hoisted the gavel one and one-half inches, then let it fall. " 'Journed," croaked Senator Pogue.

Jill Kernan's Senate office was purposely deco-rated not to betray the fact that its tenant was a woman, but the clues were there. A shocking orange umbrella hung on the hall tree and to one side of the large window stood an easel and sketch pad. These were unusual accessories for a senator. Watercolor pads accumulated behind a file cabinet at a rate of about a foot per year. Measuring the height of the stack could tell one the length of her term in office.

"Get your presentation together, Vern," Jill was saying into the phone. "The old fossils are going to listen to my 'egghead scientist friend,' so make it good."

Jill was sitting on the couch in her office with her feet on the coffee table. She almost never used the large walnut desk which dominated the room.

"Yes, Vern," Jill replied. "Next week's regular meeting." She nodded vigorously at Dr. Graham's reply. "Hell, yes, Vern. I know that. I've got Tannenbaum locked up. Carson is slipping into my pocket. More will start coming around after you've talked to the Committee. You're a respected Nobel Laureate in physical chemistry. A male one. It's the dinosaur brigade that has to be rolled over."

Jill sprang to her feet and began to pace her office, the long phone cord trailing behind her. "Don't worry about that," she said. "I'm having lunch with my Air Force 'spy' today. First, I'll get the man I want to command all picked out. *Then* I'll start leaning a little here and there. We can bring irresistible pressure on the Joint Chiefs gradually. We won't have to *sell* them anything. When I get this on the jungle telegraph, a ton of brass and gold braid will line up waiting for the store to open."

She paused. "How's that?" Jill laughed heartily as Graham repeated. "Depends on what you're selling, Vern. Don't worry. By the time it comes down to a vote on funding the military will be *insisting* on your tornado project."

Chapter 3

Chelsey Quincannon was a female. Even her baggy Air Force flight suit couldn't hide the fact. 1LT C.L. Quincannon, USAF, career officer and qualified all-weather jet fighter pilot, with a degree in aircraft engineering was a woman first and a flier second.

Chelsey was assigned to the Air Force Systems Command at Andrews AFB. She was very popular with military hostesses. She was very beautiful, very intelligent, and absolutely charming. Between her duties and the Washington social circuit she knew the best of the brass, on duty and off. She was Senator Kernan's Air Force "spy."

Chelsey smiled across the luncheon table, rubbing the back of her neck as she adjusted the collar of her blouse. Civilian clothes had seemed to be in order for lunch with a friend in the Senate.

Over long-necked clams they had begun working their way down a list of potential commanders for the Anti-Tornado Program. Jill had researched a likely group of senior officers. Chelsey was on first-name terms with most of them. She knew them all by their reputations inside the military—truths rarely revealed to any civilian.

"Cantwell's not your man," Chelsey said flatly. "Made brigadier off the bottom of the list. That's about as good as off the wall. Physically, he's a wreck. As a commander he's too rigid—usually about foolish things."

Jill crossed the name off her list.

The lady Senator and the lady Air Force Officer were tucked away at a quiet table in the dining room of the Mayflower Hotel. A gusting wind spattered rain against the nearby windows.

The dessert arrived as Jill was saying, "That leaves us with Commander Jarrell, Captain Pellourne, and Colonel Hammer. We put Colonel Harrison on hold."

Chelsey dipped into the banana cream pie, chewed thoughtfully, with pursed lips. "Jarrell's a young hot-shot. Has combat experience and is a fairly steady flight leader. He could probably handle this, but I think he ought to have more seasoning before he takes an experimental program command. He's kind of brash.

"Now, Pellourne has brains but lacks guts. He's

never held a command job, although he likes to let
on that he has. He can't handle people. He ruffles
them up because he don't know crap about how to
smooth out feathers.

"That leaves us with Harrison and Hammer. Of
the two, I'd pick Hammer. Now, Harrison is all
right. He has just as good a record as Hammer, but
he lacks color. I mean, he's—oh, hell—just not
appetizing. I think the pigeon you need for the slot
needs to be a guy with a certain amount of dash.
Hammer is a good-looking dog, photographs well,
and is a gifted bullshitter. Thinks on his feet—you
know—you can't stump him."

"Yes," Jill replied. The commander should cap-
ture the public's imagination. Taxpayers have to be
on our side. Until the program proves out, good ol'
Senator Thundercheeks Thurlow will fight it. The
first squadron commander will have to be one hell of
a leader. We can't afford mistakes. How does Hammer stack up on that score?"

"Dreamy." Chelsey looked fondly at the
paneled wall of the dining room. "You've looked
at his Officer Effectiveness Reports as a unit commander in Southeast Asia? Strike records. Decorations. *Very* low losses among his own pilots.
Number of individual missions he led in person?
Then, the NVA put a quarter-million piastres price
on his head. All of that?"

Jill nodded as Chelsey went on. "It's all true.
You know? All straight. None of it is glossed up.
Sometimes buddies will make an officer's record
look good on paper to salve his feelings if he's not
earning as many medals as somebody else. His own

people call him Colonel Dan. That's a sign of respect you don't find very often in our business."

"Sounds like our man," Jill said. "I'll put out
some other feelers from the technical end of
things."

"One other thing you should know," Chelsey
said evenly. "I'm a good kid, but I can be bought."

"I don't follow you," Jill said.

"I have a price for giving you all this information." Chelsey measured the words evenly, "I
want to be one of the first pilots in the program."

Jill sat back in her chair abruptly. "Hell. I hadn't
thought about that, Chelsey!"

"You can swing it," Chelsey replied flatly.
"I'm damned tired of what I have to go through to
keep up my flying hours. I'm rump-sprung from
piloting a desk at Andrews. This here tornado-
killing romp is the slot I've been waiting for. I'm
qualified and I *can* do the job. Besides, sister, I
won't settle for less."

Dr. Graham paused a moment to discover if there
was an elaboration or addition to the question from
someone else on the Committee. He looked up and
down the table.

"The point is, ladies and gentlemen, that the
Achilles' heel of the tornado is right here in its
head, to mix a metaphor, where the funnel cloud
blends into the overcast." He indicated the spot on
the projected photograph slide with his light-wand.
"Although a tremendous amount of thermal energy
is driving the whirlwind, it is being attenuated upward from this focal point. I am sure that a rela-

tively small bomb detonated in or near the head will interrupt the flow long enough to cause a general breakup of the vortex structure.''

''And just how *big*,'' Senator Thurlow asked sharply, ''is this here 'relatively small?' '' Sam Thurlow stomped down hard on the words, *''relatively small.''*

Dr. Graham adjusted his steel-rimmed glasses with a practiced motion. ''It might weigh as much as five tons, Senator. That isn't a good description, though, because it wouldn't be like a conventional high-explosive bomb. I'll go into that after we're better acquainted with the enemy we seek to destroy with such a bomb.''

He flashed a new slide onto the screen. ''The funnel cloud of a tornado may be several hundred meters in diameter and thousands of feet tall. What we see here is condensed water vapor whirling in the vortex. Near the bottom are dirt and debris sucked up from the ground. This detritus spirals upward with the air mass until it spins away and falls back down, outside the vortex structure.''

''Like Dorothy's house in 'The Wizard of Oz,'' Jill said brightly.

Dr. Graham smiled, ''Yes, Senator Kernan, that's an apt illustration.''

As Senator Thurlow groaned softly and started to speak Chairman Pogue shushed loudly while adjusting his hearing aid.

Graham outlined the funnel with the arrow of his light-wand. ''What determines the shape of the tornado vortex is the place where the wind isn't. Like the eye of a hurricane, a tornado is a low pressure region around which the air is rotating as it spirals up to higher levels. The upward, that is to say vertical, velocity may be in excess of one hundred fifty miles per hour, but the rotational velocity of the wind in the spiral vortex is much greater. It ranges from three to six hundred miles per hour, depending on the size of the tornado. The dangerous part of the whirlwind, of course, is what touches the ground. The dynamic pressure of the wind at this point against, say, a building, can exceed one thousand pounds per square foot. If that doesn't knock it down, the building can be exploded by its own internal air pressure as the eye of the vortex passes over it.''

Dr. Graham smiled at Jill as he adjusted his glasses. ''So, you see, Senator Kernan, Dorothy's house would more probably be blown up than picked up by a tornado.''

Senator Tannenbaum interrupted. ''Excuse me, Dr. Graham. How does such a monster get started? What makes it so powerful? We've all seen dust devils and similar whirlwinds; why don't they turn into tornadoes?''

''It's a matter of the thermal energy available, Senator. Now, I can't give you a cram course in thermodynamics and meteorology in two minutes, but I've prepared a simple illustration that may enable you to understand some of the physical forces at work in a tornado.

''In this next slide, we see a simple thermal updraft which has been transformed into a small whirlwind. It starts from this layer of air which has been heated by contact with the sun-warmed ground. Because the density of the heated air is less than the surrounding air mass it rises in a column like a hot-air balloon. It continues to rise and cool until it reaches an equilibrium level. Here, the density of the rising air is the same as the density of the ambient air mass.

"The rising air current spins into a vortex as it goes up. Like water running down a drain, it prefers to spin because that is the mode of least effort. This poetic explanation is not scientifically satisfactory though. Converging streamlined flow is unstable and will change into rotational flow at the slightest provocation. In the case of convective air movement, the rotation of the Earth provides enough provocation, enough perturbation of the rising column, to get the job done. The Coriolis force that deflects an artillery shell in flight actually occurs because the Earth rotates under the projectile while it is in flight. In free air or water the Coriolis force is so strong and significant that virtually every natural vortex spins in the same direction—with the Earth's rotation—counter-clockwise in the northern hemisphere and clockwise in the southern.

"Since the dust devil's only source of energy is that thin layer of warm air at the ground surface, it can't grow any larger than the ones we have all seen. Though these can grow to several meters in diameter and as much as a thousand feet tall in a desert landscape, once they run out of warm air they dissipate. A patch of vegetation, a green field, or a small body of water will often kill such a disturbance.

"Though driven by similar forces, the tornado has

a vastly larger supply of thermal energy to feed
upon.

"Consider this next slide, showing conditions in
the wake of an advancing cold front of the type that
generates massive thunderstorms. This storm is
powered by the release of tremendous flows of
thermal energy from the moisture-bearing air powered by billions of horsepower, to draw a crude
comparison.

"Such a storm results from a peculiar stratifica-
tion of the air. In the midwestern states, for example,
moist air flowing from the Gulf is often superimposed by a layer of warm, dry air coming off the
Rockies. On top of this is a layer of really cold air
of normal density, sweeping down from Canada.
The bouyant warm air below makes the interface an
extremely unstable air mass with a lot of violent
vertical air motion in large eddies. In the general
pattern of the resulting circulation we see warm air
rising in thunderheads, where the moisture con-
denses and throws off more heat while cool air
flows down in front of the disturbance mass. Back
there in the turbulent cloud formations, the simple
rotating motion of the Earth can start any one of these
big updrafts spinning—often more than one. Tornadoes in pairs are fairly common.

"Once started upward through its breach of the
cold air stratum, the spinning column of air is self-
perpetuating. The vortex first appears as a short,
dark cone descending from the cloud layer over-
head. As more and more air rushes in, the funnel
lengthens. By the time it touches ground, the
fully-developed tornado's destructive potential is

already at work. Unlike the tiny dust devil feeding on a thin layer of heated surface air, the tornado has an ocean of warm, moist air, from which it can draw power.

"To stop a tornado, we must halt this cycle. This can be done with a bomb designed to generate more heat energy than blast energy. First, the fireball would raise the temperature of a large mass of air rapidly enough to destroy the convective motion. Second, the pressure wave, the blast's shock wave, would disrupt the vortex flow in the neck of the funnel below."

Jill spoke up quickly. This series of questions had to be asked, as well as answered, correctly. "Dr. Graham," she said, "How can a bomb of this sort and size be used without posing serious danger to the people and real estate in the immediate area? What are the hazards of the operation you describe?"

"About the same as throwing your hat at a landslide."

Dr. Graham caught Jill's admonishing stare as Senator Thurlow gathered himself for an acerb comment.

"I do not mean to be facetious. The bomb would explode at an altitude of several thousand feet over an area already being ravaged by a tornado. No one nearby, spared the tornado's destruction, would be subject to another threat just as deadly. The bomb will be proximity-fused to detonate above a pre-set altitude. Sensors in the fuse mechanism would not allow it to explode below some optimum altitude where a tornado head would not likely exist. Additionally, the bomb casing would not be metallic.

Instead, a plastic material which would be con-
sumed by the blast heat rather than shattering into
fragments can be used. Pyrolon fills the bill nicely
in that respect.

"The shock wave of a thermal blast, as you likely
know, is not as severe as that of conventional explosives. The explosion occurs slightly more slowly.
A heavy Pyrolon casing would control the size and
shape of such a blast in much the same way as the
casing of a claymore mine."

Senator Carson held up his hand. He had a college degree in physics and felt a certain rapport with
the scientific community—"kinship" was the
word he often used. The fact that he had no experience in the field whatsoever—his post-graduate
degree was in law, which had led into politics—
never deterred him from chatty expressions of his
"kinship" with the hard sciences.

Dr. Graham nodded toward Carson. "Suppose,"
Carson said thoughtfully, "that these safety
mechanisms fail, Dr. Graham, and the bomb
plummets to earth. Dangerous, what?"

Dr Graham smiled. "Excellent point, Senator.
The bombing run, as I see it, should approach the
tornado from the upwind side, so the bomb trajectory will intersect the ground and terminate in the
path of the tornado. Then, the bomb itself, *if* it
failed to detonate, would fall in the path of immediate destruction. Whether or not it detonated
there would be less important than at any other
physical point. However, it will be constituted of
explosives and arming devices which will *not* be
detonated by shock impact, and the Pyrolon casing

will eliminate the possibility of its being detonated
by friction heat. Of course, a solid projectile of that
much mass, falling from several thousand feet,
makes a good-sized hole in the ground. But what is
one more hole in the wake of a tornado?''

"Excellently thought out, Doctor,'' Carson said
redundantly. "You seem to have covered the bases
on that one. Now, then, I'd like to know more
about this Pyrolon bomb casing you propose—''

Senator Thurlow interrupted, "How is it, sir,
that you are so well-acquainted with Pyrolon, a
highly classified material being tested by the Department of Defense? The kind of usage *you* describe for it is known only to a few highly placed
civilian officials and a handful of science officers in
the U.S. Air Force.'' Thurlow arched an eyebrow
at Dr. Graham as if to say, "Gotcha, Mr. Egghead.''

Chapter 4

Jill looked anxiously at Graham. Thurlow was raising a question of a possible breach of Defense Department security. Here more than anywhere else appearance was as important as the facts.

"Touché, Senator Thurlow," Dr. Graham said with a grin. "You have gone and pinked this old egghead in a vital spot."

Thurlow frowned.

Graham smiled more. "I have the utmost respect for your regard toward matters of security, Senator, and your question shows a healthy concern with perspicuous inquiry into such areas."

Thurlow chuckled. He sensed that he had somehow lost his supposed advantage. When uncertain,

Thurlow chuckled good-naturedly and began to re-
group his attack. "Perspicuous, indeed, sir," he
chuckled. "That, sir, should be obvious."

"Senator Thurlow, while it is not the sort of
personal history that is widely publicized, I was
privileged to be a participant in the *invention* of
Pyrolon, and performed most of the polymerization
work in the development of the material."

"I understand, sir," Thurlow replied. Then in an
insinuating tone he continued, "You have, should
we say, an *interest* in Pyrolon?"

"If my understanding of your implication is not,
shall we say, presumptuous," Graham said sharply,
"please allow me to correct in advance any mis-
apprehension. I have no *vested* interest in Pyrolon as far as defense work is concerned. That is to
say, there is *no* opportunity for me to reap personal
gain from its use by the government."

"Is the government use of Pyrolon connected at
present, in *any* way, with civilian companies in
which you have an interest?" Thurlow's face was
creased by a smile. "In fact," he added quickly,
"*is* the government now making any use of Pyrolon?"

"You know that it is, Senator," Graham said
flatly.

"Sir?"

"Two days ago, a Department of Defense
courier delivered to your office a current report on
the trial usage of Pyrolon casings in Project Kickapoo, which is currently being carried out at Aber-
deen Proving Ground by a joint Army and Air Force
research command. While the report itself may have

been a little technical, I'm sure it was effectively boiled down for you by the DOD engineer you had lunch with yesterday. I'm sure, Senator Thurlow, that you are as up-to-date on Pyrolon as I am.''

Thurlow put on a friendly face. ''Welllllll—''

''*Especially*,'' Graham deliberately interrupted, viciously stepping on Thurlow's folksy comeback, ''since I authored the report.''

''Welllll,'' Thurlow drawled, unruffled. ''You're certainly right about that, and I retract any unkindness you may have inferred from my remarks. . . . *(This son-of-a-bitch has really got his ear to the ground. . . . Knew about me having lunch with Creaghmiller, too. Well, you can't fart in Washington without* somebody *smelling it.)* . . . Just for the sake of argument, Dr. Graham, could you give us a brief rundown on Pyrolon and the potential shown in Project Kickapoo?''

''I'd be delighted, Senator. I'll assume that all the members of the Committee have a security clearance for this, and, in light of the tornado project under consideration can be said to have a need to know . . .'' He looked questioningly at Thurlow, then Senator Pogue.

Thurlow gave a hearty phlegmy laugh. ''Proceed, sir.''

''Pyrolon,'' Dr. Graham said, ''Is a stable long-chain polymer under nearly every condition except sudden high temperature, such as occurs in an explosion. A sharp heat blast turns Pyrolon directly from a solid to a vapor.

''Now, in its solid state it has a texture, appearance, density-mass, and weight that reminds one of

both polyethylene and polystyrene. It is more di-
mensionally stable than polystyrene while retaining
the excellent resistance to stress-induced fracturing
of polyethylene. Plainly speaking, Pyrolon is hard
to bend or deform, but will tolerate a great deal of
bending or deformation before it breaks. It can be
blow-molded or formed by pressure injection mold-
ing, and is easily machined to five-mil tolerances.

"Pyrolon's heat-blast vaporization, mechanical
properties in common with other cheaply produced
polymers, and easy machining with unsophisticated
machine tools make it an ideal candidate for military projectile casings. Like conventional metal cartridge and shell casings, the Pyrolon casing con-
tains the propellant charge until the propellant
explodes, then, unlike conventional casings, it also
disappears."

Lacking a prepared visual presentation or materials for his impromptu explanation of Pyrolon,
Vernon Graham suddenly lost his composed manner and used his hands dramatically. He moved his
arms animatedly to draw pictures in the air. In front
of the lectern, he imitated shell casings with his
forearm, transformed his fists into artillery shells,
and made his fingers into machine gun bullets.

"Now you see, a Pyrolon casing goes up along
with the propellant charge. You don't have to ex-
tract or eject the empty round.

"The use of such casings permits simplification
and economy in the weapon's action by eliminating
the need for extractor and ejector phases. At the
same time, this allows utilization of less sophisticated machinery to feed rounds into the firing cham-

ber. Although the firing pin and bolt face are no longer protected from blowback and will erode very rapidly, the benefits far outweigh the inconvenience and minor costs of changing bolts and breech faces as part of the weapons' periodic maintenance. The weapons will be simpler, more efficient, and less expensive than heretofore.

"Now, just to bring you up to date on Project Kickapoo . . . Two problems exist with automatic and crew served weapons which are mounted in mobile carriers. To illustrate these simply, consider the tank and the aircraft. Similar problems exist in both, but I want to be brief.

"Rapid fire of the turret gun in a tank accumulates spent shell casings inside the tank, and these have to be jettisoned in some practical way which does not interfere with the operational capacity of the tank itself. In a supersonic aircraft, on the other hand, the spent rounds *must* be jettisoned. The possibility exists in the jet fighter's automatic gun systems that there will be duds and misfires. The possibility of a dud round falling into the pile of hot brass ejected by—say—a .50 caliber gun or a 20mm cannon simply cannot be allowed. The hot brass casings can set it off. Further, you can't simply dump the spent casings overside into a supersonic slipstream, because they will trail alongside the aircraft and rip up the skin. The jettison system currently in use is very expensive and space-consuming." Graham riveted Thurlow with a sharp look. "And, it is very highly classified, Senator Thurlow. I shan't discuss it here. Regardless of your individual security clearances, none of you have a need-to-know basis for receiving such information.

"The purpose of Project Kickapoo is the operational testing of Pyrolon shell and cartridge casings in these two kinds of critical applications and use areas. The objective is to eventually adopt Pyrolon as a casing material for all military uses, from the automatic rifle on up to the 175mm howitzer. Future applications include possible utilization in the windshield structures of armor-piercing shells, cone detonators in shaped-charge rockets, an improved propellant increment system which would replace the rather old-fashioned powder bags used in 210mm artillery and in 8-inch naval rifles. Well—the list goes on, and it would bore you, I'm sure."

There was a general pause, but no questions were forthcoming on Project Kickapoo, either because the Committee members had not prepared themselves to discuss it or because they were digesting the possibilities which Dr. Graham had outlined.

Senator Thurlow broke the silence. "Well, Dr. Graham, this Pyrolon stuff sounds like a wonderful invention. If I understand you correctly, it just sits there and behaves itself until something it's wrapped around explodes; then it does like the wonderful one-hoss shay.—Poof!" He spread his hands suddenly.

The laughter that rippled around the table lightened the mood. Graham had tried to explain a great deal of technical information in a very short time.

Senator Carson dove in lightly with another question. "Would you clarify Dr. Graham, if there is *any* liquid state of Pyrolon in these usages. I mean, does it simply sublime from a solid to a gas at a given temperature—like carbon dioxide?''

Graham chewed his lip. ''Essentially, you're right, Senator. Sublime isn't really the word I would use, since Pyrolon is not a crystalline structure at all. I would say, rather, that it could be said to have a 'temperature of vaporization' at which it is transformed as you suggest. Actually, this is a temperature *range*, but it is a very small range. Finally, the absence of residue—the 'clean' transformation of state is a characteristic that is particularly desirable for the use we have discussed. For instance, a similar system—a so-called 'disposable shell casing'—has been tested in the self-propelled 105mm howitzer, but the dangerous fumes generated accumulate in the crew compartment each time the breech is opened. The toxic danger of the fumes is so great that the shooting efficiency of the gun is rendered nearly useless. There are no such problems with Pyrolon.''

Senator Thurlow spoke up hesitantly, as if amazed. ''Do you *really* mean,'' he rumbled, ''that you ain't gonna make *any* money off the government from this Pyrolon stuff? No *royalties?* No *residual licensing fees?* He stared at Vernon Graham and sucked in a lungful of air for the final thrust. ''*Nothing?*'' The word crackled through the room. Thurlow settled back for the riposte.

''I assure you,'' Graham said, fighting down the hostility which rushed into his tone, ''That any use made of Pyrolon by the Department of Defense is quite legally and clearly franchised and licensed to the government—at *no cost*—Did you get that,

Senator?—clearly? *No cost* to government for the use of the basic patents. *No one* will make any *royalties* from it. Later uses by private industry may—or may not, depending on the derivation, research level, application, and a lot of other things— involve payment against the patents. As government use now stands, *I* won't make a crying dime out of Pyrolon, nor will anyone else—except for the salary that I might earn. Note that I said *earn*, Senator. Now, then, if the Defense Department should decide, for some reason, to use *paperweights* made out of the damned stuff, then I just *might* make a couple dollars out of it, *if* I'm not working for the government at the time. Does that answer your question, Senator?''

"Admirably, sir. Admirably," Thurlew deferred.

"Once and for all?" Graham insisted.

"Most assuredly. . . . *(Well I found his hot button. Question his integrity and honesty and he just gets all pissed off and unstuck. Either he's feeling guilty as sin about something or he's the cleanest, straightest son-of-a-bitch I've ever seen in the hallowed halls of our nation's capitol.)* . . . I was not questioning your integrity or honesty, Dr. Graham. I apologize if I gave that impression. . . . *(We'll see, scientist. We'll see.)* . . ." Thurlow scribbled something on his scratch pad, tore off the sheet, and put it in his pocket.

Jill Kernan bit her tongue to keep from saying what she was thinking. *The hell you weren't, you old bastard.*

Graham's eyes were blazing. "Would the Senator

like to see documentation in support of my statements on this matter?"

Thurlow waved his hand, "I trust you, Dr. Graham. The ladies and gentlemen of this respected committee trust you I'm sure. However, if your project is funded for research, you'll have to file paperwork to the effect that you are receiving no personal gain other than your pay as a consulting scientific expert."

"I *understand* that, Senator."

"Wellllll," Thurlow drawled. "I didn't think otherwise. If you'll pardon my saying so, Dr. Graham, you *do* have an honest face."

A few members of the Committee giggled nervously.

Chapter 5

While Graham and Thurlow eyed each other Jill leaped at the opportunity to re-direct the inquiry. "Dr. Graham? How certain are you that one bomb will kill our run-of-the-mill tornado?"

"Hmmmmm." Graham pulled himself together. "Though not a matter of certainty, Senator Kernan, the probability is that one bomb would do the job. I think it most advisable that the aircraft delivering the bomb be followed closely by a second and a third plane. Should the first be a little off target or score a partial hit—drift of the tornado during the time the bomb is traveling could cause that—there should definitely be immediate backup delivery capability. With a computer-controlled autopilot attack system, the probability of a miss would be quite small—the head of a tornado is a hell of a big target—but we have to consider the primary need, which is to kill the tornado within a matter of minutes after it is fully formed.''

There were rustlings from the head of the table; sounds like parchment rubbing on sandpaper. Senator Pogue was going to speak. He cleared his throat. ''Dr. Graham, ah'm very much *dis*turbed by the grave danger to which you would expose our highly, and I might add, expensively trained, military pilots. Ah was born and reared in twister country and the very sight of those devils a-stormin' across the prairie sends brave men down into the cellar like unto a badger diving into his hole when the hound-dog approacheth. Giants brawling in the skies; that's what we called tornadoes when I was a boy. And, you'd best get out of their way or they'll squash you like a bug.''

''Excellent point, Chairman Pogue. An excellent point.'' Jill quickly stepped in before Senator Pogue could get his oratory machinery cranked up. She turned toward Graham. ''How dangerous is the pilots' job?''

''I am concerned, too, Senator. The danger to the pilot and his aircraft in the turbulent air can only be minimized, not eliminated. The apparent solution is to penetrate the storm structure as slightly as possible, remaining in the turbulent field as briefly as possible. Pitch-bombing, perfected in World War II, is ideally suited to this purpose. Let me show you a series of simulation slides of a typical bomb run against a tornado.'' Graham restarted his automatic projector.

"As you see, the attacking plane comes in low, running just under the speed of sound, and arcs up clear of the storm system *while* its bomb is lobbing toward the target at the tornado's head. By the time the bomb explodes, the flier who delivered it is above the clouds. Note that the typical attack path shown on this overlay composite brings the bomber no closer than two miles to the target, a relatively safe distance, even in the case of a very large tornado."

Senator Jill Kernan added her remark, adroitly timed to set up patriotic inertia. "I wouldn't expect our flying officers to shrink from this kind of combat. They are brave and able men, and courage is the rule with them rather than the exception."

"You are absolutely right, Senator Kernan," chimed in Thurlow. We all have ample reason, as legislators and as common God-fearing citizens, to be proud of our air services. They are the best-trained and best-equipped in the world. They are the finest pilots on the face of the planet, fearless in their vigilance and ever ready to protect freedom without regard for their personal safety—"

"Are your remarks going anywhere," Jill snapped, "or are you just making a speech?"

"Here, *here*, chirped Senator Pogue as he loudly rapped the gavel. "Committee members will not squabble in this chamber!"

My apologies," Senator Thurlow serenaded. "We are all a bit drawn, perhaps. I have one last question for Dr. Graham, and then I suggest we recess for luncheon."

Vernon Graham nodded his assent to the question.

Senator Pogue rubbed his stomach. "Go ahead and ask him, Sam," he said to Thurlow.

"Is it all worth it?" asked Senator Thurlow.

Jill Kernan started as though jabbed with something sharp.

"I'm afraid I don't follow you," Graham said.

"Suppose," Senator Thurlow said thoughtfully, gazing at the ceiling, "just suppose this project of yours *could* eliminate *all* the tornadoes that take place in a given year's time. How much help would that be to the country? I know it would afford our combat pilots, or at least a select group of them, practice, but how much help would it be in terms of cash money? Can you give it to me in dollars and cents?" Thurlow sat back.

He's coming around, Jill thought excitedly. *The old bastard's coming around to* my *side, whether he realizes it or not. Maybe he's just trying to trap Vern into a specific statement of statistics, which he knows is impossible, so he can accuse us of* "pronosticatin'," *but he's* really *backing up* my *argument.*

"I think I understand your concern, Senator" Graham said measuredly. You deal with budgets, averages, mean expenditure levels, and cost-per-item on a vast scale. Against this you must weigh abstractions such as the dollar value of a human life, the dictates of global arms balance, and the harsh practicalities of determining what the electorate has the heart and will to accomodate. If you'll lower the lights, I have one more slide series to show you."

Graham threw a dozen brutal pictures on the

screen in rapid succession. They graphically showed a tornado's destruction from the general to the painfully specific. A wide aerial view of an entire town reduced to rubble and kindling by a tornado was followed by a mockingly intact chimney. The pictures snapped into grim life on the screen, pulling the Senators into the personal tragedy of tornado damage. Dr. Graham left the last picture on for a full five seconds. It was a closeup of a wrinkled old woman sitting on a rocking chair amidst the ruins of a farmhouse. Her face was blank and dirty; two streaks marked where tears had washed the dirt away.

The committee members were barely breathing.

Jill Kernan was shaking: perspiration lined her forehead. She was startled at her reaction to the slides. *The pictures are strong stuff,* she thought, *but I've never had* this *kind of heebie-jeebies before. If I had, I'd sure as hell remember it—wouldn't I?* She fought to maintain a placid look of sincere interest. She hoped no one would notice.

Senator Sam Thurlow noticed, though. He eyed Jill sharply for a moment, without her knowing, and scribbled a note on the scratch pad in front of him. He tore off the page and put it in his pocket.

Vern Graham had caught Jill's reaction, too, and it puzzled him. He had carefully planned this part of the presentation with a colleague in motivational research, but Jill had been ready for this. She would have asked the question if Thurlow hadn't.

The haunting tornado victim was replaced by a neat statistical abstract chart and Graham began to speak in a flat businesslike manner. "Based on av-

erages over the previous five-year period, this is
what we have harvested from our tornado crop *each
year* in the United States of America.

"Seven hundred thirty-one separate tornadoes.
Six hundred ninety-two killed. Nearly one *billion*
dollars in property damage, not counting direct
damage to crops. Remember that these are averages,
ladies and gentlemen. Tornadoes are more caprici-
ous than these figures indicate. The 'giants brawling
in the skies,' as Chairman Pogue has so aptly called
them, are deceptive in their destruction—elusive of
analysis by mere cold arithmetic.

"The U.S. Department of Commerce has been
keeping records of tornado damage since 1916.
Their record year was 1965 when nine hundred fifteen tornadoes killed two hundred ninety-nine
people. Yet, in 1925, there were only one hundred
nineteen tornadoes, but the death toll was seven
hundred ninety-four.

Graham adjusted his glasses and looked at his
notes. "On the 18th of March in 1925, the most
deadly tornado in our history swept through Missouri, Illinois, and Indiana. During that one day, six
hundred eighty-nine Americans died. I don't have
statistical data on the property damage and cost in
crops destroyed. I know only that six hundred
eighty-nine persons were killed that day.

"In 1925, we did not possess the aircraft or
technology to declare war on tornadoes. Today,
however, we have both. And, wonder of seren-
dipitous wonders, these tools can be used to fight
tornadoes in a program that will save the taxpayers
more money than it costs them. It is not even neces-

sary to put a dollar value on a single human life to arrive at the mathematical relationship. Property damage averted will justify the cost. The lives saved are just a bonus.''

Senator Thurlow, interjected ''That is only true, sir, *if* your program works.''

Vernon Graham faced them squarely. ''That's what I'm here for, Senator, to pass my battered hat for a megabuck or so. I crave a boon from the guardians of the public purse in the fond and fervent hope that a vicious form of natural disaster *can be struck down*. I say it can, if we have the courage. Gentlemen of the Senate, from the day the land first came up from the sea, these giants have walked the earth. They raged in the wake of the first thunderstorms, ripping apart the primeval forests. Masters of the land before men lived there, they seemed enraged at the intrusion of fragile creatures of flesh.

''And still they strike at random, without warning, at any hour of the day or night. They leave behind them smashed homes, broken lives, the mutilated dead. In the paths of these blind old furies, strong men are as helpless and fearful as children. Their awesome strength has always been accepted as unchallengeable.

''Until now. Gentlemen, you hold in your hands the power to end this terror. Like the shepherd boy David, we must place a smooth stone in our sling and pitch it at the giant's head.''

My God, thought Graham, *they've got* me *jawboning with the mandible of an ass. Five pounds of rhetoric in a two-pound bag . . .*

Sam Thurlow stopped in the men's lounge on his way to lunch. He knew his fellow committeemen would be there, since it had been a rather long session that morning.

"This here Graham fella is one hell of a spell-binder, isn't he?" Thurlow asked of no one in particular. He "harumphed" quietly, not certain that he had been noticed.

Senator Erwin Culpepper Pogue noisily finished washing his face and spluttered into a towel. He blew his nose, also rather noisily, and studied himself in the mirror. He was a rail-thin old gentleman of Victorian demeanor that did not completely gloss over the fact that he was a red-necked politician at heart. The skin on his face was pale and translucent as fine parchment vellum. It was only slightly wrinkled in spite of his considerable age. Senator Pogue took good care of himself.

He carefully combed his sparse white hair and eyed Thurlow in the mirror. "Ah wouldn't worry about it too much, Sam," he said. "Graham's not from yo'r state, so he can't run for yo'r office."

"God damn it, Erwin!" Thurlow snapped. "That's not what I meant, and you know it."

"Just funnin', Sam; just funnin'."

"Graham does have a powerful sales technique," remarked Jake Tannenbaum, as he hitched up his pants and re-buttoned his vest across his ample midriff. "I like what he has to say. That is, it makes—you should pardon the expression—good, practical sense. Hearing practical talk has become a luxury for me since I went into politics."

"That's what I mean," Thurlow said. "It only makes sense if it *works*. I sure as hell don't want to get in further than my knees until we know it *works.*"

Erwin Pogue smiled and screwed his hearing aid more tightly into his ear. "Theory never was yo'r long suit, Sam. How we gonna know? How we gonna find out if it *works* unless we give it a whirl? You speak for yourself, but I'd hate like hell for somebody else to make it *work*, after we'd killed the proposal."

"Well, that's what I *mean*, Erwin," Thurlow replied. Even if Graham is a bleeding-heart liberal, he seems to have a good idea, here. But he's been listening to that Little Miss Smart Aleck girl from out west. His *application* is too ambitious. I mean, federal programs can draw a hell of a lot of fire, especially if they run wild and get the news people all stirred up."

Senator Pogue pulled at his ear thoughtfully. "What's the alternative, Sam?"

Thurlow stepped lightly into the conversation, testing the water as he went. "Well, you got to understand that I'm not opposed to this tornado-killing scheme *on the merits of the proposition*. It's a fine idea. But, it rankles me for people to just *assume* that things like this *have* to be *federal* programs.

"The fearless white knight of states' rights takes up his shield, eh, Sam?" said Tannenbaum.

"Carpetbagger!" Pogue remarked absently.

"Hold on, boys," Thurlow said. "I'm serious about this. Think for a minute. What is our normal posture of reaction in a natural disaster? Flood, fire, hurricane, blizzard, earthquake, *and* tornado?"

"We know, Sam—" Tannenbaum enjoyed bait-ing Thurlow— "Mobilize the National Guard. Provide transport. Evacuate victims. Protect property. Direct traffic. We know."

"Of course," Pogue interjected. "Local folks know the local situation. They're familiar with the ground. Our militia, 'scuse me, National Guard are local folks. They're right there. They can be on the job in less than an hour's notice."

Thurlow smacked his fist into the palm of his hand. *"That's my point!* It appears to me that this tornado-abatement idea should be combined with the Air National Guard operations in *states that have tornadoes!* Sixty percent of our military is in reserve components. That's what makes us or breaks us in terms of readiness. And, I can tell you for sure, maintaining flight proficiency is a hell of a lot tougher for an Air National Guard pilot that it is for an Air Force full-timer. We can man the program at state level and make it work just as well, *and cheaper,* than any active armed services branch."

*"Un-*fortunately," Tannenbaum said, "tornados don't come addressed and delivered to a specific state. You still have to have very sophisticated radar interlocks, communications that link into a single, national net, and a very sophisticated computer net to make something like this work."

"Aw, hell," Thurlow replied. "We're all tied in with the National Guard Bureau, and with each adjoining state. Why, one or two tornado bases in each state that has tornado problems will give you a faster reaction time than a whole scatter of them attached to *selected* Air Force bases. Little Miz Kernan doesn't know that, though. You see, they don't have tornadoes in *California*. That's why she's so hot to ride the coat-tails of this thing as a *Department of Defense operation*. Her, on the look out for that good ol' national welfare, is just the mash of this situation. What she hopes to distill off of it is party control in the next congress. I don't like that. She ain't in my party. Her governor won't like it, either. He *is* in my party. *He'll* wonder why she's fritterin' around with tornadoes, when she *should* be in there punching for the salt-water plants that farmers *need—right now—*in her own state.'' Thurlow wagged his finger toward the ceiling— ominously. ''I tell you, boys, there's more to that lady's motivation than meets the eye.''

''There's something to what you say,'' Tannenbaum admitted. ''But, I'll have to study it more before I draw any voting conclusions. I'm not sure, for example, that National Guard pilots are trained up to a fine enough edge to pull this sort of duty. National Guard people maintain a certain level of readiness—yes. Regular functions and annual Training keep them up to date and competent up to a point. But you can't *expect* a Guard unit to be in crack shape. You can expect them to have trained people ready to mobilize on a few hours' notice. Take notice, Sam, I said ready to *mobilize*, not ready for *combat*.''

Thurlow started to reply heatedly but Tannenbaum held up his hand and shushed him before he could get started. ''Sam, don't go telling me about the Guard's finest units. I know that some Guard battalions have passed Training Tests that few active Army battalions could. Don't tell me about the exceptional. I'm not talking exceptional; I'm talking everyday reality. You know damned well that a new program or piece of hardware can *not* have its operation and procedure established by turning the development over to a military reserve component. Now, that's just the facts of life, Sam.''

"Harrrrrrrrrumph,'' Pogue interrupted. "Ah cannot speak for the states *you* two gentlemen represent. But ah *can* tell you that *our* boys down home have always given a good account of themselves when called to take up the sword and rid our land of the dread alarms of—''

"Hold on, Erwin,'' Tannenbaum said good-naturedly. "We're not marching off to subdue the heathen or something. We're just going to bomb some tornadoes.''

"You *politicians* are getting off the point,'' Thurlow rumbled darkly. "The *point* is, we are involved with a *regional* problem that only requires widespread attention for maybe seven months a year. Now, if that isn't a problem for *local* military reaction and control, I don't know what is. If you have Air Force personnel operate this thing what the hell do they do with themselves when tornadoes are *out of season?* They keep right on drawing pay and allowances. That's what!''

"They also,'' Tannenbaum said with forcefulness, "go right on maintaining a *combat-ready* proficiency. They learn to do their jobs better and with fewer fuckups. And,'' he arched an eyebrow, "when a combat pilot fucks up, it usually kills him. Think about that, Sam.''

"But, goddamit,'' Thurlow sputtered. "Think of the goddam *money* that's involved.''

Tannenbaum laughed. Funny you should mention it, Sam, but I was just thinking of that very thing.''

"Eh? Thurlow said, suddenly off guard.

"I don't suppose your reaction here has anything to do with the fact that you happen to be a brigadier general in your own state's National Guard, does it? Are you—I don't mean to offend—hungry for some of that *federal* money for your state's military?'' Tannenbaum smiled blandly.

"It has to do," Thurlow said huffily, "with the *fact* that my own service position *puts* me in a position to know what I'm talking about on this point. I say, 'skunk her.' That's what I say. But, from a standpoint of harmony, if you boys want to go along with her, I will too—at least temporarily. In the end, though, you'll see that I'm right about this. Y'all depend on it." He paused.

"Today's Tuesday, isn't it?" he asked, suddenly calm again.

"I believe it is," Tannenbaum said. "Why?"

"If they have baked ham, *without yams*, again today, I'm going to raise hell."

"Baked ham is not something I think about very much," Tannenbaum replied.

Chapter 6

"I won't do it!" roared Colonel Daniel Hammer. "By God, *I won't do it!*" He stomped up and down his boss's office. "Dammit, Joe," Hammer raged. "Some son-of-a-bitch is fucking me around. I'm due for my first star, and I won't get it if they keep jacking me around!"

Hammer's boss puffed thoughtfully on his pipe. "I can't help it, Dan. It's out of my hands." He shrugged and spread his hands, as if to show there was nothing in them but the pipe he was holding. Major General Joe Stewart was the Commanding General of Air Force Systems Command HQ at Andrews AFB. As one of Daniel Hammer's oldest friends, he really did wish there was something he could do.

Hammer seemed not to hear. He stopped in front of General Stewart's desk and ticked off his gripes on his fingers. "They set me down at Langley to organize a wing consolidation. That's a job that calls for a brigadier, and they generally give you the star if you put together the assignment.

"I get the wing in shape and the next thing I know, I'm back at Andrews flying a desk on this goddam Logistics Evaluation Team. *Now,* they want to put me to shooing flies away from the buckle on the Corn Belt. Bombing twisters, by God, Joe— *bombing twisters!* Me in command of an experimental squadron! They can stick it! I'm due for a wing command. I've punched the tickets—group command, ground exec, air exec. This makes no sense at all, Joe. I'm being robbed and all you can do is sit there and puff on that damned pipe!"

"Well." General Stewart raised his eyebrows. "There's no point in busting a blood vessel about it, Dan. They're considering you as the military commander for a joint-service pilot program of tactical anti-tornado bombing. It's not like they've cut orders on you or anything. But, when I get the word directly from the Assistant Secretary for Research and Development, it looks like you're going."

Hammer flopped his large frame into a chair. "Shit, Joe! It's not fair."

"True, true," Stewart agreed.

"Well, what can we do about it?"

"Me," General Stewart said matter-of-factly, "I can do nothing about it. I have a memo from the Assistant Secretary to *not* reassign you until they decide if you are the man they want to command the twister outfit.''

"You could give me a couple days off. If I pop over to the Pentagon, shake a few hands, twist a few arms, maybe I can worm my way out of this thing. What do you say?''

"Sure," Stewart replied. "I'll even give you a letter to Jack Winthrop, asking him to help you out, but make sure he shreds it in front of you after he's read it.''

Hammer leaped to his feet. "That's a deal!''

There was a gentle rap on the door of Stewart's office. Dan Hammer noticed that the door was already ajar.

"Come in," Stewart said.

"Here are those materials consumption recaps from Logistics at Wright-Patterson, General.''

"Thank you, Lieutenant Quincannon. You know Colonel Hammer, I believe.''

"Sure enough." Hammer answered for her. "How's tricks, Chelsey?''

Chelsey smiled her widest grin. "Swingin', Colonel Dan; just swingin'. I didn't know you were at Andrews," she said innocently.

"Been here three weeks now," Hammer replied. "Logistics Evaluation Team." He pronounced the words as though they didn't taste good.

"An' you never looked me up?" Chelsey asked petulantly.

"Welllll," Hammer excused himself, "the team was pretty screwed up. Lots of whipping into shape needed, you know. And the admin records— Christ!—you should have seen the records. So, I had to do some hiring and firing before I got the people I wanted where I wanted them.''

Joe Stewart chuckled audibly.

''All right, Joe,'' Hammer said ominously.

''We've been talking about cooking, Chelsey,'' Stewart said by way of explanation. ''You know. What's sauce for the goose is sauce for the gander. That sort of thing.''

Chelsey Quincannon laughed, heartily and loudly, but with an unmistakeable sexiness.

''You were listening,'' Hammer accused.

''You left the door open,'' Chelsey countered.

''It was closed when I came in,'' Hammer said.

''Old building,'' she said. ''The doors in this place all swing.''

''That's not all,'' Hammer grumped.

''All right. All right,'' Stewart said. ''Chelsey brings in more information than she takes away. This isn't the goddam War Room, you know. We're not plotting global strategy or anything.''

''But—'' Hammer began.

''Point is, Colonel Hammer,'' Stewart cut him off, ''Chelsey works for *me*, and *I'm* satisfied with her work.''

Chelsey smiled at Hammer, as charmingly as possible. ''You going to be hanging around for a while, Colonel Dan?''

Hammer looked at Stewart.

Stewart looked at his watch. ''Day's about shot, Dan. Why don't you pick up that paper work from me in the morning and head uptown then? Get a fresh start on it.''

Hammer turned to Chelsey. ''You have any plans this evening?'' he asked.

Chelsey cocked her head to one side. "Just hangin' around, Colonel Dan. Just hangin' around."

"Well," he said, "let's have some dinner and talk about it."

"I'll bring you up to date on all the gossip," she said. "But, it'll take me a couple more hours to finish up here."

"That's fine," Hammer said. "I've got an ass-kicking conference with my team leaders at four. I want to ruin their appetites for dinner so they'll remember what I say."

Chelsey grinned. "Well, don't hurt your own appetites, Colonel Dan. Pick me up back here about five or so. You have transportation?"

Hammer nodded. "Got a sedan assigned to me."

"Good," she said. "Turn your driver loose. Let him get his own—"

"Dinner." interjected General Stewart. He guffawed loudly.

Chelsey Quincannon lived on the top floor of a civilian apartment complex. The windows caught the reflection of the rising sun off the Chesapeake Bay.

Sunrise was still a half-hour in the future as Dan Hammer stood at Chelsey's bedroom window. Traffic was already moving steadily on the parkway below. The clear air made the cars and trucks seem so close that Hammer felt as though he could reach out with an enormous godlike hand and pick them up like toys. Aircraft wafted soundlessly in the distance. As they climbed, each of them would wink brightly as the dawn light flashed on its metal skin.

Chelsey stretched and opened her eyes. She was

a little startled to see a man standing in her bedroom. It was the exception instead of the rule, but it
was not a rare or momentous occasion for her to
wake up with someone beside her. She studied him
for several minutes, without his being aware that
she was awake or watching him.

In the luminous dawn light his tanned skin
looked very pale and translucent. White cigarette
smoke eddied around him. She liked the way the
light fell on his body. It had the aspect of a Vermeer, except then she couldn't recall that Vermeer
had ever done figure studies of muscular men. With
Dan Hammer she was a lot more aware of the sex-
ual difference between them than the color difference. That was a matter of genetics that meant nothing in the relationship. Wondering if he felt the same
way, she chuckled, low in the back of her throat.

He turned sharply. "Joy in the morning?" he
asked, smiling.

She shrugged luxuriously. "No," she fibbed. "I
just had a funny thought about how different a colonel looks in his underwear."

Hammer snorted. "Everybody does, baby. I'd
rather see you in your underwear any day, but if we
didn't wear those cute little airplane-driver suits
during the day the Air Force would never get its two
dollars' worth from us."

"You're up early." She shifted the subject
slightly. "You always get up this early, or just
when you're with me?"

"Habit of a lifetime," Hammer said. "Maybe
someday we can spend about two weeks in bed to
see if you can break me of the habit."

"Mmmmmm." She stretched again, working her naked body about halfway out of the covers. "Besides that what were you thinking about?" she asked.

He moved away from the window and sat down on the edge of the bed, sharing the cigarette with Chelsey. "Actually," he said, "I was thinking about all those mornings when I've gotten up at dawn, or before, or at 3:30 in the morning, or whatever—right on back to the first one."

She plumped the pillows and sat up. "First what?"

"First morning, you sex fiend. What do you think?"

"Tell me about it," she said.

"It's all a blur," he said. "Everything melts together. In the pre-dawn there's white wooden barracks with fire-lights outside the doors. I'm an enlisted man, then a dumb-ass second lieutenant. What sticks in my mind the most, I guess, is the attitude about waking up early. When I was younger, it was a hell of a struggle. On my days off I'd be furious about waking up at dawn. Later on, when I was married, it was still the same way. I'd pussyfoot around the house and read the paper and do a lot of thinking. I wouldn't wake her up, though; she hated to get up early.

"Now, I sort of savor waking up at dawn. Gives me a chance to look at the world when it's not looking back. Maybe our senses get sharper as we get older. Some people say that, you know. But, maybe we just have enough data accumulated so we can catch on quicker, see through things to the conclusion of the job." He paused. "Hell! I don't know."

"You going to re-marry anytime?" Chelsey asked.

Hammer laughed abruptly. "Why? You want to settle down with me?"

"Not me," she said. "What, and spoil it all? Love is like banana cream pie, sugar. You get it all the time and you don't appreciate it any more."

"Well, I'm not a diabetic," he said, and rolled her over backwards across the bed.

She squealed in mock surprise and rolled away, but swiveled back alongside him. "Watch the cigarette," she said. "You burn a hole in my sheets and I'll spank your ass with your own boot."

"Hmph," he said. "To answer your question, Lieutenant; I have no immediate plans to re-marry. An officer can be excused of one divorce on the grounds that the lady did not like military life. A second one renders him suspect in terms of maturity and ability to maintain interpersonal relationships. That is to say, it tends to be a career-buster."

"Like the tornado command?" she asked. "You're looking at that as a career-buster, too?"

"Shit," Hammer said disgustedly. "We went all over that at dinner. I'm ready for my wing command. And I'll get my wing despite those fuckers buried in the bowels of the bureaucracy who want to bury *me* in a cornfield somewhere bombing twisters. Don't get me started on that again. I'm goddam bitter about it, and they haven't even stuck me with it yet."

"Well," she countered, "here's something that will make you feel better."

"Sure," he said as he began stalking her across the bed.

"Don't be silly—yet." She held up her hand. "Example. When World War II started, Dwight Eisenhower had what he thought was a logical and high ambition. He wanted to command a tank regiment. And—boy!—was he pissed off when they wouldn't give it to him. Think about it. If he had gotten his way he would have done all right. On VJ Day he would have been just another fat-ass old colonel or brigadier."

"So?" Hammer shrugged. "You weren't even alive during World War II, and I was—well—very young. I had to read about it later in the history books. Given my choice in the matter, I would have preferred to spend World War II in bed with you. I mean, as long as we're dealing in fantasy, how's that one?"

"Now, listen close," Chelsey said solemnly. "The wing command that you're suffering for is swell, *but*, the tornado command is a high-profile job. You make the airplane end of it work and you'll *sure* get your star *and* lots of publicity. Which do you want more, your 'tank regiment' or a spot in the bullpen from which they will pick the next Air Force Chief of Staff?"

"Groovy," Hammer said sarcastically. "Porcupines making love, baby. You approach that one —correction, *I* approach that one the same way as getting married again—very carefully. What if it all turns to shit, somehow? I *know* I'm on solid ground with a wing command. What if I flunk the tornado job? Or, what if some shithead senator or undersecretary just sinks it because he had stomach gas that day? Then what?''

"Sheee-it!" Chelsey was genuinely angry, now. She jumped to her feet and strutted around the foot of the bed, moving every muscle of her magnificent body with each step. "If you're worried about that —I mean, *really* worried about it—then you ain't the Dan Hammer *I* know. You get things *done*, sugar. I can count all the officers *I've* ever *heard* of on one hand—and have a lot of these left over—" she wagged a finger at him "—who got the guts and brains *you* do when it comes down to the nitty-gritty. You know the time to stop with the *briefing* and the *operations planning conferences* and *get it on*. You can put the people and planes together and *make it work*."

Hammer grinned lopsidedly. He dropped to one knee and clasped his hands imploringly. "I love you," he said. "Will you be my press agent?"

"Bullshit!" she snapped. Then, she couldn't keep from laughing. "A colonel, in his underwear kneeling in my bedroom. I'd tell this one to the secretarial pool, but they'd never believe it."

"Besides," he said, "you're very discreet." He got up.

"I am, at that," she said. "See if the coffee is ready, while I put something on." She paused. "You did start the coffee, didn't you?"

"Indeed, I did, ma'am," he replied as he started for the kitchen. "Don't get too complicated with what you put on," he called from the hallway. "We have time to patch up our differences and have breakfast on base.''

Chelsey grinned at the window. The sun was coming up through the haze over the horizon. *''Yeah,''* she said.

That afternoon, over cocktails with Jill Kernan, Chelsey was saying, "You can call it eavesdropping if you want. I call it 'casual G-2 improvement.' ''

Jill waved her swizzle stick impatiently. "I take back the eavesdropping part. Then what did he say?"

"Well." Chelsey paused to smile broadly as she debated with herself. "When he found out the tornado outfit was to have one-third of the active pilots *female* officers, he really hit the roof. You wouldn't believe the *language!*"

"I can believe it," Jill said calmly. "So, he doesn't want the job?"

"Doesn't want the job? He's kickin' and bitin' and clawin' to get out of it."

"Good," Jill said satisfiedly. "That's the kind of man the job has to have. Otherwise, some small-minded yahoo will be able to cripple it."

"But, look here, Jill," Chelsey said, "this is really kind of a dirty deal. I mean, he *is* due for brigadier, and he deserves to get it."

Jill arched an eyebrow. "Where is Colonel Hammer, now, my dear?"

"Well," Chelsey replied, "he took off up Suitland Parkway with his afterburners roaring and his tail surfaces on fire."

Jill nodded. "Exactly. Even as we sit here, holed up in this friendly establishment—plotting darkly —Colonel Hammer is holed up in some officers' club bar with one or more of his colleagues from the Pentagon—likewise plotting darkly. Nonsense." She snapped her fingers to emphasize the point. A waiter appeared from nowhere. "Oh, dear," Jill said, "I didn't mean— Oh, well. Bring us two more. Anyway, Chelsey, it's the fortunes of war. I *need* Daniel Hammer for this program. The more I learn about him, the more convinced I become. He's the bull for the job. When he's through bellowing and stomping he'll see the good of the program. And as soon as the program is off the ground, Hammer will get his star. I'll see to that."

"Unless something goes haywire," Chelsey said evenly.

"Hmph!" Jill said. Not this time. Hammer's only worried about his little old star. If *I* blow it on this tornado project. I'll never hold public office again." Jill looked at her watch. "I have to get to a press conference. I swear, if I live through this, I'm going to flake out on a beach somewhere for two whole weeks."

Chelsey winked. "Do a little fact-finding tour, huh?"

"Fact-finding. Manhunt. R and R. Trapsetting. Motelling. Call it what you want. I've got to get a little rest and put myself back together."

"I think you're right, after all," Chelsey said.

"About a little hanky-panky at a resort?" Jill asked.

Chelsey smiled noncommitally. "Dan Hammer's definitely the bull for the job."

Jill looked perplexed as Chelsey leaned back, loose and laughing.

Chapter 7

After a long wrangle in committee, funding was approved for a research and development program to test Dr. Vernon Graham's tornado-killing theory.

Frankford Arsenal would supply the experimental bombs. The Lockheed "skonk works" would modify Navy F-4 Phantom II aircraft. The Navy would then prove the bombs on the Pacific Test Range. Dr. Graham would co-ordinate the nuts and bolts end of the project. Assembling a joint Air Force/Navy experimental squadron to carry out the first attacks on "live" tornadoes would be up to Colonel D. Hammer.

A military jet transport set down at Offutt AFB, Nebraska. As he got off the plane, an outraged

Colonel Daniel Hammer was handed a set of orders
with the ink still damp on them. He quickly read the
orders, muttering unspeakable oaths to himself.
Then, he took off his forty-dollar uniform hat and
threw it down on the concrete apron as hard as he
could. He might have stomped on it, had not a
thunderstruck junior officer snatched it up and—
quivering—handed it back to him. Hammer ran
his fingers through salt-and-pepper hair, as he
jammed the hat back on his head. The orders were
crumpled with a single savage gesture. He loped off
across the runway, his long legs chewing up the
distance between his plane and the headquarters
building.

Before Colonel Hammer's plane departed Offutt
for McConnell, he had time to get on the Autovan
and place a call to Senator Kernan in Washington,
D.C. In a four minute call, Colonel Daniel Hammer
managed to fit in three unsavory suggestions about
Jill's ancestry, five remarks of a distinctly "male
chauvinist/sexist pig" nature, and used fourteen
phrases of a sufficiently profane magnitude to make
the switchboard monitor—a grizzled master sergeant—wince visibly.

That was the kind of man Jill Kernan wanted in
command of the Anti-Tornado Project.

Senator Jill Kernan pushed her project through
Congress. She scoured the cloakrooms for support,
wheedling and cajoling. When that didn't work, she
bullied and brow-beat. She threw cocktail parties
for apathetic legislators, big butter-and-egg men
from the news media, and various third-assistant
undersecretaries who had little real authority but

were capable of expediting paperwork for one project while bogging down another in endless red tape.

She ground out releases for the press. She wrote articles and gave interviews. She faced down leonine old colleagues on the floor of the Senate when they sought to shut her up. And, she tacked a zig-zag course through a political fire storm in her own state.

The party-liners were being forced to watch federal funds go to an anti-tornado program. Funds that *could* have gone to California if the state's Junior Senator had taken less interest in the price of corn in Kansas and put more fight into the pork barrel. They had no idea of the fierce drive that moved Jill Kernan to wage war on tornadoes. She, herself, did not fully understand the thirst in her for vengeance which swept her relentlessly on to the final conclusion of her battle against the killer whirlwinds.

Now, after three months of push and pull, the first three-plane flight of the Anti-Tornado Program was being made operational. A bone-weary Jill Kernan opened one wall panel in her office and switched on the television. Opening a second panel, she fixed herself a drink. As sunset lengthened shadows on the lawn outside her office window, she kicked off her shoes and settled on the couch to watch the news.

Jill put her feet up on the coffee table, sipped her drink, and turned up the sound.

"*. . . following a sharp statement issued today by the founding Chairman. Charges previously levelled at the Baron are quite false, he declared in an exclusive interview, and form part of a vicious* *whispering campaign designed to cover up and cloak the power-play organized among slack-minded board members by the management of Malthus Enterprises . . ."*

"Hmmf!" Jill said aloud. *"Chickenshit board members* is what he *meant,"* she interjected as the newscaster paused for breath.

" *. . . Secretary Ian Griphon of that con-glomerate could not be reached for comment, and is believed to be out of the country, pending an Internal Revenue Service investigation of circumstances sur-rounding a recent stock split by Malthus. While . . ."*

Frankford was satisfied that the new bombs were safely up to operational standards. Dr. Graham had accepted the Navy's refinements on firing techniques after extensive testing at sea.

Five kill tests were authorized. Scheduled to begin in early March, they would take on the first tornado close enough to hit. McConnell AFB, in the heart of "Tornado Alley," had been picked for the test operation. If the unit was successful it would be the first of a nation-wide network of anti-tornado stations.

The second-hand Phantom II's modified for the simulated training attacks at sea were refurbished and groomed for the first kills. If the program was successful, Giant-Killer might obtain more appro-priate, or at least more up-to-date aircraft than the aging F-4J's.

The bomb, a 150 cm.-diameter sphere would be carried internally. It couldn't just hang under an aircraft moving at supersonic speeds. With a weight of 4500 kilograms, it also had to be close to the aircraft's center of gravity so the plane would not pitch wildly at the moment of release. The bomb bay was in the big fuselage cavity, replacing some of the fuel tank area.

The bomb bay doors were coupled to an internal catapult sling, womblike around the bomb and equipped with powerful hydraulic actuators. When the doors opened, the big egg kicked gently out of its nest and hung under the aircraft during the attack run at subsonic speed. As the plane pulled up, centrifugal force gained on the velocity of the aircraft. Released, the bomb hurtled from the aircraft's belly at a tangent to the arc of the pull-up path.

The bomb was connected to the fire-control computer through an umbilical cable. Through the cable, the bomb and the computer "talked" to each other. Bomb fuze calibrations, altitude settings, and timer overrides, fed into the bomb's control cell at the beginning of the attack run, could be updated and refined right up to the instant of release. Since the bomb was designed to produce a spherical burst of white-hot gas, the igniter-booster was embedded in the center of a special propellant charge with a wallop equivalent to two tons of TNT. Concentrically surrounding this, within the 10 cm.-thick Pyrolon shell, was a high-density *thermogen* of Dr. Graham's own formulation which would flash-burn in the atmosphere with as much heat as three tons of Napalm.

'' . . . *pooh-poohed the rumor that he stands to gross over two million from the movie-TV-cassette rights to his latest novel,* 'With a Finger in My Ear.'

*Columnist B.J. Truncheon talked with author
Fraidmann in his lush Beverly Hills office complex,
nerve-center for product lines franchised from his
busy pen. '. . . is utter nonsense. I write for the
sake of the work itself, out of a restless urge to
create. I'm only a simple storyteller at heart. I'm
really a babe in the woods in the business world. If it
wasn't for my manager, I'd . . .'''*

Cuss 'em, thought Jill. Are they going to cover
the story or aren't they?

The first flight would be at Wichita by now.
They had taken off this morning from NAS North
Island at San Diego, moving their own planes to
McConnell: First Lieutenant Chelsey Quincannon
and Captain Lee Bates of the Air Force, and
Lieutenant Peter Selby of the Navy.

Selby was the best qualified flier in the bunch.
Twenty-six years old, he had been flying since he
was eleven. A fast look at his Form 20 and his 214
easily explained his exceptionally high score in the
pitch-bombing trials. He had been assigned to
Giant-Killer from the Department of Defense
Parachute Test Facility at El Centro. Dirty-weather
flying seemed to be his forte. While still in high
school, he had ridden several storms to new soaring
records. Selby was considered heir apparent to the
legendary "Thunderstorm Maxie," one of Ger-
many's early sailplane pioneers. Selby had bailed
out with every ejection device and popped every
parachute the military had ever thought about. He
had logged over a thousand jumps—two hundred
and sixty-five of them in experimental devices.

Flight Two had completed foul weather flight

training at Pease AFB and was moving into the
same pitch-bombing phase just completed by Flight
One. Dan Hammer had chosen well: Major Doris
Polanski from Air Force, Lieutenant Commander
Harry Rosenthal from Navy, and a colorful Marine
pilot, Captain Stanley Lemm. The Marine Corps
had put up such a howl that the manning table had
been modified to accomodate pilots from the
USMC on a direct ratio-of-strength basis.

*'' . . . which makes the second Pulitzer Prize
for the burly novelist.*

*"We all know the story of Jack the Giant-Killer.
Here now is correspondent Hanklin C. Atlano with
an update on JILL the Giant-Killer. Hank . . ."*

*"Thank you, Hal. Today should be a happy one
for Senator Jill Kernan of California. For several
months she has led an uphill fight to establish a
tornado-killing program which would utilize
combat-trained pilots from all the military services
in a project designed to virtually eliminate the
threat of tornadoes. The project was officially
launched today by its civilian director, Dr. Vernon
Graham, Nobel Laureate in Chemistry, and, the
project's first military commander, much-
decorated Vietnam ace Colonel Daniel Hammer of
the U.S. Air Force. The two posed for photo-
graphers alongside a new type of thermal device
which Dr. Graham has designed to break up tornado winds. After a ribbon-cutting ceremony, both
men held a news conference at McConnell AFB,
near Wichita, Kansas, where, the experimental
phase of the project will be located. Operation
Giant-Killer, as it has been dubbed, will, it is*

hoped, prevent millions of dollars of tornado dam-
age annually, and save hundreds of lives.

   "While Dr. Graham fielded technical questions
from reporters and science writers, Colonel Ham-
mer outlined the military applications of Operation
Giant-Killer, pointing out that the project involves
practically no cost to the taxpayer, since it affords a
productive program by which military pilots will
maintain their flying proficiency at required readi-
ness levels and still be of continuing service to the
American public.

   "Colonel Hammer expressed pride at being
selected as the first commander of the joint force,
and hailed the project as a milestone in the co-
operation he feels should be more frequently prac-
ticed between the military services and elected civi-
lian authorities.

   "Reached earlier in Washington, Senator Ker-
nan lauded the qualifications of Dr. Graham and
Colonel Hammer in . . ."

   The crucial phase of Operation Giant-Killer was
launched quite literally with a bang.

   They had no sooner uncrated Dr. Graham's new
eggs than the tornado watch sounded the first alert.
One plane was serviced, armed, and on the line,
and another was almost ready when the word came
that something was brewing in a thunderstorm
which had rolled over the southern edge of Kansas.
Soon, a full-grown twister was striding northeast—
toward Wichita. The roaring wind could be heard
for more than fifteen miles and was still building.

   Colonel Hammer was gone in the AirMobile van

and couldn't be raised on the radio. The van was to be used as a rolling command post, and for triangulation and commo relay. Dan Hammer was grooming the rough edges off the crew and getting the bugs out of the equipment.

There wasn't time to wait for the Colonel. As Lt. Selby climbed into the cockpit of the readied Phantom, he was giving orders for a second plane to be put in the air as a backup. The crew chief buckled him in and hooked up his commo and sensing lines. He handed Selby a T.W.X. just off the teletype.

SELBY: LEADER: JILLFLIGHT ONE
918TH TEST SQUADRON JOX(DOVJ) 76566
MCCONNELL AFB

JILL THE GIANT-KILLER WISHES YOU GODSPEED AND GOOD HUNTING.

KERNAN
WASHINGTON

Selby grinned. "She couldn't have timed it better, even if she had known what was cooking. This just come in?"

The Senior Sergeant nodded. "Personal messages to everyone in Giant-Killer Command. You should have seen the one she sent to Colonel Dan." The sergeant was shouting over the scream of the plane's engine as he unhooked his workstand.

Selby guffawed and waved at the man on the ground as the canopy closed and locked. He pushed the throttle and began to creep across the apron.

Strong gusts were rocking the plane as Selby

taxied to the end of the runway. He eyed the wind patterns traced by racing dust clouds which whirled across the airfield. With calm detachment he pondered his chances for getting the aircraft off the ground without being killed and decided on a straight shot with all the power available. "Jill-One Leader to tower. Time's a-wastin', control. I'm going while I can."

"Tower to Jill-One Leader. Go, Leader. You're the only guy in the barrel."

Selby turned into the rising wind and kicked in the after-burners. The plane went up like a rocket, riding a shaft of flame and clawing for altitude. The jet blast momentarily muffled the sound of the charging enemy, but Selby could soon hear through the plane's canopy and his own helmet. As soon as he was above the trees and had eyeball contact with the horizon, he could see the tornado. He was already flying through air as heavy as any he had ever handled.

He swung out to flank the giant, gaining altitude and distance as he banked through a long lazy-eight that brought him back into the general line of the tornado's advance.

"Jill-One Leader to Giant-Killer Control. Do you have a new heading on target?"

There was a long silence. Finally, a scratchy voice over background noise — very faint. "Break-break. Uh — Jill-One, this is Giant-Killer Ten. Giant-Killer Six talking. Control not reading you, but we copy traffic on both. Hold your pattern, sailor. The Ten computer is thinking about you and enemy. Six over."

Giant-Killer Ten was the call-sign for the commo

van, which was also ground net control, and Six was the squadron commander's personal call-sign. Selby was relieved to hear Colonel Hammer's voice on the radio.

"Roger, Six. I copy. Glad to hear from you. Glad the Air Force came to town. Jill-One over."

"Roger, Jill-One," Hammer said. "We're about twenty clicks west of Giant-Killer Control. The monster is veering our way now. Our bearing to Control is seven-two. Target bearing five-two. Fill your bank and come to attack heading of two-two-niner for straight-in intercept vector. Computer confirm; two-two-niner. Target distance from Giant-Killer Control—reference Giant-Killer Control—seven-one air miles. Target speed, two-four knots. Max altitude forty-one hundred—four-one-zero-zero feet. *And*, computer confirm; attack speed five-two-zero—five-two-zero knots—at altitude two-four-zero-zero feet. Jill-One do you copy computer confirm? Over."

"This is Jill-One. I copy data, Six, and now store input." Selby repeated the figures and he punched them up into input storage, ready to release into the attack computer on board his aircraft. "Input now stored, Six. Request Computer Analysis Update. Over."

"Roger, Jill-One. CompAn Update working. Your input is go, Jill-One. CompAn readout confirms. Insert attack program as you come to bearing two-two-niner. Over."

"Roger, Six. Jill-One on attack bearing. Input now inserted to on-board program. Do I have your permission to attack this baby?"

Hammer's voice came out as a strangled laugh.

"That's a rodge, Jill-One. Readout shows me right in the path of destruction. You're driving the airplane, sailor. Go for his throat. Giant-Killer Six out."

Selby steadied in under the churning clouds, found his course overlay as he dropped a sonic boom on the little town of Millerton. He idly thought that the residents probably didn't even notice the shock wave.

In his soup-screen reticle loomed the most formidable foe he had ever faced; a whirling black giant five hundred meters in diameter and over twelve hundred meters tall. He throttled down, dropping to the prescribed speed and altitude. He tapped his mike twice and left it open as he counted down. "Jill-One to Giant-Killer net. Coming up. Coming up, now. Crossing the I.P. . . . Mark! Locking on auto attack at mark. . . . Three, . . . two, . . . one—mark!" A second's pause. "Damned rough air. I can see the wings flapping on this old bird. *Egg away!* And, away we go! Up! Up! Up! Orville and Wilbur, pull me up!''

Selby's plane dug a furrow through the clouds as the bomb departed on a long, rising trajectory. Instead of rolling out in the sunlight on top, he continued to loop over. He came back down farther away in the swilly weather, but still in full view of the tornado. The bomb, buried in the monster's head, had just exploded.

On the Harper-to-Viola road, Colonel Daniel Hammer's men had pulled the AirMobile van into a shallow creek, in the shelter of a road bridge. As

soon as radar confirmed the shot, they piled out of
the van into knee-deep water to watch the tornado
blow up—or to take cover under the bridge if it
didn't.

The tornado was less than a mile down the road,
tearing up billboards and trees as it came. It spewed
out the fragments the way a farmer broadcasts grass
seed. The sound was deafening. The whole world
was filled with the thunder of wind and the tortured
ripping of solid objects as they were swallowed in
destruction.

The men on the ground saw the fireball rip a hot
spot in the overcast. Seconds later, the shock wave
rocked the van and rattled loose gear inside it.

Someone shouted something that couldn't possibly be heard above the roaring, dirt-laden wind, but
they all saw that the bomb-shot was right on the
money.

With mounting concern, Hammer waited, wondering if the twister could blow down a stone
bridge. Was it working? Then, as though someone
had dropped a plug into a drain, the head of the
vortex broke up into a cluster of furious eddies. The
whirlwind ran down like a dying top. The full-
blown funnel cloud simply evaporated.

Suddenly, it was quiet. The wind was still violent, but compared to the din of a moment ago, the
world seemed abruptly silent.

Colonel Hammer and his well-disciplined ground
commo crew dissolved into a mob of cheering,
laughing madmen, hugging and pummeling each
other as they were engulfed in a harmless cloud of
whirling dust.

Lieutenant Selby, also intoxicated with delight, buzzed over them at treetop level, pushing the speed of sound. He waggled his wings impudently and pulled up into a series of three tight victory rolls.

Moments later, at the base, a beaming Dr. Graham gripped Selby's hand warmly. " . . . Beautiful piece of work, son. I think we're onto something here. Let's have a little de-briefing over in the maintenance shed. There's some champagne flowing already."

Selby was grinning. "Thank you, sir. We ought to go a little slow until Colonel Dan gets here. Shouldn't be more than a few minutes, though. You know, he had that commo van out there right under the twister. Practically *inside* it!"

Graham nodded. "I know. I know." He frowned. "What was he doing out there, anyway? I heard the radio traffic."

"I'm afraid to ask him," Selby replied. "But, when we crack the second bottle, I probably will." He frowned. "I think I *know* what he was doing, anyway. He's the kind of guy I figured he was.

Chapter 8

Operation Giant-Killer's second kill was made under less impromptu conditions. All three of the modified Phantoms were ready on the flight line when the alert sounded. Chelsey Quincannon drew the lead spot on the flight. On the radio net, her enthusiastic running chatter had ears ringing for a week afterward. But, she steadied right down when she attacked the tornado, laying in a "textbook" shot that destroyed the giant before it could travel a dozen miles from its original touchdown and sighting.

Colonel Hammer was already slogging through the Paperwork Battle. He had three planes in Jill-Flight-One. Period. No alternate aircraft. No backup equipment except Vern Graham's clutch of eggs. He didn't care at all for the idea of having to send up a two-plane flight against a tornado if the third one was down for maintenance.

Dan Hammer was under enormous pressure to succeed with the mission. A week didn't go by without a flock of civilians settling down to roost at McConnell for a couple of days. Scientists, congressmen, senators, engineers from Defense, liaison observers, and tribes of meteorologists from the National Oceanic and Atmospheric Administration.

Occasionally, there would be a dense little knot of observers from Project Kickapoo. They would pop in out of nowhere, furiously measure various properties of the Pyrolon bomb casings—density, thickness, temperature, surface microscopy—and just as suddenly disappear.

To add to these, his familiar tribulations, there was a goofy young engineer from Defense who had been attached to the project to do fatigue studies on the aircraft. Craven Creaghmiller was his name. Whenever Hammer would ask him for definite data about wear-and-tear on the planes, he would dash off to his cubbyhole office in the maintenance shed, muttering things like, "revised data," "newly graphed tensile patterns," and "bending resistance flexion," without ever really answering the question.

While Creaghmiller typed endless reports and maintained endless graphs taped to his office walls, Colonel Hammer depended on the opinions of his combat-seasoned ground NCOs as to the durability status of the planes. They simplistically suggested that the solution to the Creaghmiller irritation was to take him out behind the hangars and have him shot.

Much as Hammer enjoyed that particular fantasy, he had to leave Creaghmiller alone. Creaghmiller didn't work for Hammer. Hammer could boot him off the project—could boot him off the base— could have him arrested if he wished. But, he would have to really have something that would stick. And, Creaghmiller never actually *did* anything to warrant any kind of reprimand. He was just a meddler. He was underfoot. He always seemed to be mocking, but never *did* anything you could really pin on him.

Jill-Two's arrival at the McConnell anti-tornado station was still over two weeks away. It looked like a hairy time ahead. Until Jill-Two was operational the crew chiefs wouldn't have a chance to do really thorough teardowns and maintenance. Also, their arrival would take some of the pressure off Jill-One pilots.

In the meantime, Hammer played the game he knew well. He was the kind of officer who, though discipline-conscious, commands respect and obedience by force of leadership and example rather than by rank or title.

He soon scuttled inter-service rivalry. It had been one of his early targets, since he knew well it could cripple a joint-service operation quicker than anything else.

He got himself checked out on the modified Phantom II and brushed up until he could fly it as

well as any of his pilots. He participated in the
pitch-bombing simulations in thunderstorms and
"proved up" to all the people in his command;
essential exercise for the man who has to issue the
orders, then take it in the shorts if he is wrong.

When the third kill mission came, Jill-Two had
not yet arrived, and one of Hammer's aging fighters
was torn down for some dental work on its turbine.

Dan Hammer had a bad feeling about the situation. He told himself it was combat fatigue from the
Paperwork Battle. Ignoring intuition, he sent up the
two-plane flight. One of the bombs detonated too
deeply into the vortex to make a clean kill. The
tornado was a "hopper," dancing back and forth
erratically. The second bomb was laid on accurately, but the giant sidestepped the shot while the
bomb was in trajectory. The tornado was crippled,
but it still took out a long strip of Nebraska real
estate before dying.

Colonel Hammer and Vern Graham had been
raising hell in Washington for five more modified
Phantoms to provide backup aircraft. So far, it was
no dice. It wasn't that Washington wasn't willing,
just that in Washington *everything* takes time. Dan
Hammer knew they didn't have time. And none of
the Air Force's brand new and costly Mach 3
fighter-bombers were going to be modified until
Dr. Graham's tornado-killing theory had been for-
mally proven.

Colonel Hammer went into a "silent period." He
chatted moodily with the crew chiefs and the
ground exec. He took long meandering walks out

behind the main runway. He stayed late at his office several nights a week, surrounded with aeronautical engineering volumes, charts, overflowing ashtrays, and coffee cups.

When Jill-Two arrived at McConnell, Operation Giant-Killer was awaiting its fourth alert. A general sigh of relief was felt. The planes in Jill-One weren't exactly holding up well. The practice missions in heavy weather combined with the strains of actual kill missions were more than the Phantom II had been designed to withstand. A pervasive air of jumpiness had turned off much of the project personnel's early enthusiasm.

Abruptly, Dan Hammer christened Jill-Two "Egghead Flight," without consulting MAJ Doris Polanski, who was technically the flight leader — a breach of etiquette. He ordered an appropriate flight insignia designed and painted on the planes.

As soon as he had done that, he showed up at the air exec's office and asked for a Jill Flight plane. He was going to Washington and wanted the plane on the line by the time he had changed clothes.

Ten minutes later, he put his foot on the ladder and tossed his flight bag up into the cockpit.

Less than an hour after he set the plane down at Andrews AFB, Hammer was walking through Senator Jill Kernan's outer office.

"Colonel!" Jill Kernan's receptionist protested. "I'm telling you the truth! Senator Kernan is *not in!*"

Hammer paid no attention. He swung the door to the inner office, stepped in, looked in the dressing room, looked in the bathroom, and only then returned to the doorway.

The enraged receptionist was standing just inside the door of Jill's private office. "Colonel! This is *very* improper!"

"Betcha," Hammer remarked dryly. "Where is she?"

"In a committee hearing, but she won't be back here until four o'clock!"

"I haven't got that long," he said. "Get her on the phone."

"I'll do no such thing!"

Hammer's eyes narrowed. "Look here, chickie. I'm on the prod today. You get in my way and I'll wad you up and toss you out the window. Get the lady senator on the horn. Tell her I'm here. She can either skip out of her committee hearing and come over here for a little while, or I'll go wherever she is. I don't care which. Either way, I'm scheduled to be back at Andrews by lunch time and I need some answers first."

"Yesssssss!" the receptionist hissed into the phone. "You could call it an emergency!"

During the long pause, while some page called Jill to the phone, Dan Hammer prowled around her office as though he owned it. He spent several minutes leafing through the sketch pad on the easel. The receptionist fumed, but the phone cord was only long enough for her to get just inside the inner office. When the receptionist ducked out the door, Hammer guessed from the hushed, hoarsely whispered conversation that she was giving Jill Kernan an earful about the madman in an Air Force flight suit who had invaded her office.

"She says she'll come over here, if—" The receptionist stopped in mid-sentence.

Colonel Hammer had found the panel that covered the bar and fixed himself a drink. He raised the glass toward the receptionist. "Thank you very much" he said. "I'll wait."

"What the hell is going on here?" snapped Jill Kernan as she stalked into her office. She didn't wait for an answer.

"What the hell is going on here?" she snapped again as she entered her private office.

Daniel Hammer jumped briskly to his feet. "Good morning, ma'am." He bowed from the waist. "Just passing through, ma'am. Beg to pay my respects, ma'am."

Jill arched an eyebrow. "Hammer, are you drunk? I swear to God, I'll —"

Before she could finish the sentence, Hammer had closed the door behind her. "Stow it!" he said sharply. "That show was for the front office help. They'll be much less interested in the purpose of my visit than in my full bull-colonel act."

Jill sank wearily into the large chair behind her desk. Somehow, she felt more comfortable with four hundred pounds of walnut between her and this nut. "Dammit, Colonel," she sighed. "I'm very busy; and much as I love games I don't have time to play spy-spy with you. What is it?"

Hammer picked up the drink he had made himself and meticulously whisked away the ring left by the glass with his forefinger. "Good start, I never cared much for mincing words myself."

He laid a forefinger alongside his nose and spun

sharply to look directly at Jill. "By the way, how do you feel about having someone barge into your office and make himself at home?"

Jill sat up straight in her chair, abruptly. "I don't like it a damn' bit!" she said sharply. "Now that you mention it, I don't—"

"I don't either; not a damn' bit!" Hammer cut her short. "Nonetheless, madam legislator, I have had to steadily contend with members of your august parlimentary body dropping in at my airbase. They wander around my command as though it was their back bedroom. Thought I'd give you a dose of your own"

Jill rubbed her eyes tiredly. "*Colonel* Hammer, I have been *trying* to get as many senators as possible interested in Giant-Killer. If we expect to keep the project going, we're going to need those members' votes when the budget comes up."

"Commendable," Hammer remarked. "If we spend all our time walking your pot-bellied colleagues around the store, we won't get our job done, and there won't *be* any Giant-Killer by the time next year's budget comes along."

"Hammer," Jill said angrily, "did you come all the way to Washington to bellyache about the size of your official visitors' list?"

"No, ma'am! There's trouble in the glen, your ladyship. Vern Graham and I decided it might not be wise to go through the usual channels, lest wind of the difficulty we're having get to the wrong nose."

Jill's ears reddened and her hand flew to her own prominent nasal feature.

"No offense," Hammer said. "Figure of speech, actually.

"The problem," he continued, "is that the project is on the edge of failure. We need more equipment, more R&D people, and more operating funds, Jill. You don't mind if I call you Jill, do you?"

Jill laughed. "Why not? You've called me everything else, so far. Specifically what do you need first?"

"I've got to have more aircraft. I've been beating my head against a stone wall for weeks and getting nothing but silence and a headache.

"The Phantom II is a great little aircraft—a hell of a tough flying machine. It's beoming evident, though, that it wasn't built to stand up to tornado-force winds any more than the Wright brothers' biplane was meant to hold up in a power dive. Normal preventive maintenance will make the grade for our practice work. *But*, after we run one of these babies through a live tornado, we've *got* to pretty thoroughly tear it down. If we don't, sooner or later we're going to have a structural or control surface failure during a bombing mission. And that accident will give jolly old Senator Thurlow and his fun-loving gang of hatchet men an excuse to come after you with tar buckets and goose feathers."

"Surely tornado killing can't be rougher on the aircraft than combat flying." Jill said. "The Phantom II has held up for long stretches of hard combat work."

Hammer laughed a nasty laugh. "Thank you, Miss Pollyanna! The fact is that *any* plane has airframe failures in combat. It just doesn't show up that way, because it gets logged as enemy action. *But,* out there at Wichita, if you lose a plane—worse yet, lose a plane *and* a pilot—the problem is going to stick out like the well-known thumb. You can't hide it. They'll shut down the project as 'too dangerous.' "

"So, what do you need, Dan?" Jill's pencil was poised over her scratch pad.

"We *need* a completely new aircraft, tougher than anything that's in the air."

Jill stared at Dan Hammer as though he had lost his mind.

He shrugged. "But it takes ten to fifteen years and megabucks to get a brand-new airplane from idea to roll-out. In the meantime, I'll settle for five more modified Phantoms and some unvouchered access to replacement parts and components. We blew a mission last week because we only had two planes to send up. I've *got* to have some spare aircraft."

"I'll see what can be done," Jill said, "but don't hold your breath with election coming, they're really counting quarters."

"Don't I know it!" Hammer stormed. "Unless something breaks loose at this end, we're going to have an aircraft failure—sooner or later—that will spread one of our planes over a couple of states—one piece to each cornfield."

"Oh, don't get the wrong idea," Jill replied quickly. "I'm *more* anxious, if anything, to get Giant-Killer on a proven, permanent status before the election. If it's not running slick by the time the new congress convenes, they could cut off your funds—*all* of them—in the wink of an eye."

Hammer chuckled, low and in the back of his

throat. "You don't think I'm so big a hick, do you? You're also thinking of the prestige a successful Operation Giant-Killer could deliver to *your* re-election campaign—and your party's chances to gain control of congress next year by lining up the 'Tornado Alley' states on your side."

Jill cocked her head to one side and nodded. "There is that," she admitted.

He spun on his heel. "Oh, don't *you* get the wrong idea. It's not *your* hide I care about. You've run roughshod over me and mine. I could give a damn if you get re-elected next year. It's the project I'm thinking about. I want Operation Giant-Killer to get a fair shake. I was standing under the twister Selby blew away. I *saw* Vern Graham's theory made fact and I don't want that loudmouth Thurlow to destroy the progress we've made."

Chapter 9

"And, another thing," Hammer interjected.
"That goddam Creaghmiller! He's a consulting engineer from the Defense Department supposed to be doing stress studies. He's been in my hair since the day he got there. Can you do anything to get that son-of-a-bitch out of there before my ground crews lynch the bastard."

"Creaghmiller?" Jill was genuinely surprised.

"Yes, Creaghmiller." Hammer's irritation was plain in his voice. "It wouldn't be so bad if he would come up with something that I could use, but he's a goddam jabberer. Seems to work hard enough, but he's always around where you don't want him."

Jill was on her feet, now, and pacing around the room. "He's from Defense, you say."

"Correct, ma'am. And I get a lot less from him than he takes out of my efficiency levels."

"But—" Jill was shaken. "I haven't had any reports from him, and I—"

"This conversation," Hammer said, "is taking a very nonsensical turn. Why would *you* hear from him, anyway?"

Jill sank back into her chair. She seemed suddenly very small and frail. "Creaghmiller," she said quietly, "is supposed to be one of mine. I'm supposed to be getting information from him."

Hammer frowned. "I'm sure you have a hell of a lot of pull, lady," he huffed, "but you can't get an aircraft engineer's study from Defense like buying an evening paper. In the first place it's too technical, and in the second it's *not* legislative people's business."

Jill waved both hands in the air. "You don't understand! I knew we would eventually need a new plane for tornado-killing, but I had to have a way of getting Defense to swing the money for it. I had Vern Graham fix up a deal. Defense would send down an aircraft design engineer to study wear-and-tear on your aircraft. Defense loved the opportunity to make that kind of study of accelerated airframe fatigue. And, assuming you and your squadron produced results, I would have some technical poop to help *prove* the need for better airplanes.

"I knew the engineer was named Creaghmiller, but that's all. I never met him. He was supposed to get in touch with me once in a while through Vern

Graham. I would know roughly what his findings were and be able to lay the groundwork in committee for *getting* those appropriations as soon as we had enough ammunition to go in and ask for them.''

Jill paused, trying to collect her thoughts. ''Has Creaghmiller written up any notes?'' she asked. ''Is he keeping records? Filed any reports with Vern? *Anything?*''

''Hell! He's been wearing out typewriters making up reports, but they've all gone straight out to Defense. He keeps promising us some hard information, but we haven't seen any.''

''Then, how do you know he's sending reports to Defense?'' she asked, genuinely curious.

Hammer smiled cynically. ''I *don't*. I only know that he's sending something out to *someone,* and I'm going to find out what it is and who's getting it.''

''But, how—''

Hammer cut her off with a hard laugh. ''You think everyone who wears Uncle Sam's blue suit with the brass buttons is a yokel, don't you?''

Jill frowned, genuinely confused now.

''Military security,'' Hammer explained, ''can find out what color panties you wear, lady, and, if necessary, how often you wash them. All without your knowing anyone was even curious.''

She started to object, but he waved for silence. ''I will explain it to you, my dear,'' he said. ''In Mr. Craven Creaghmiller's desk there is a ream of paper—blank typing paper. As he uses it up, he acquires more of it. Sometimes he buys it himself. Sometimes he draws it from my Admin Sergeant, who keeps the office supplies locked up in a closet. That's what got me thinking about him. When the Air Force will give you *free* paper, why the hell would you *buy* paper and bring it to the office?''

"Unless you wanted people to think you were using less paper than you actually use," Jill finished brightly.

"Pretty clever," Hammer said. "But, then I always knew you had a devious mind. Since the first time I got a strange feeling about Mr. Creaghmiller, I have had the civilian maid who cleans his office *weigh* that stack of paper *and* shreddings in his wastebasket—each and every night. She writes down the amounts to the nearest ounce on a slip of paper. She leaves the slip of paper on my desk when she does my office. Unless there is something wrong with my arithmetic, Mr. Creaghmiller has used up approximately six hundred seventy-five sheets of paper since he has been at McConnell, but has only thrown away a little over one hundred sheets of paper. Now, I don't think he's making paper airplanes out of it, and I don't think he's stealing it.''

"I see," Jill said. She was fighting back the impulse to laugh.

"You can laugh if you want," Hammer said crankily, "but wait until I'm finished, please.

"Now," he continued, "Mr. Creaghmiller's in there typing like a madman for several hours every day. If he were a normal guy he would dictate his notes and reports on a tape machine, then have them typed up by a secretary who has just as elaborate security clearances as he does. I would of course know how much and what he has concluded.

I would know what he's found out. I would know what he *thinks* he's found out.

"Dear lady, if *you* or Vern had seen your way clear to let me in on this, I would have had some *real* security screws on Mr. Creaghmiller long ago."

"But, I didn't think—" Jill was trying to apologize.

"But, you didn't think a dumb-ass airplane driver *needed* to know your game plan. I need to know that you have a goddam spy in my command. If he'll spy for you, *God-damn it, he'll spy for other people, too!*"

"All right, Hammer!" Jill barked. "Bite it off! So I screwed up. If there's any damage, it's been done already."

"Well I guess you're right! It's not going to get any better by chewing on it." Colonel Hammer's temper was subsiding. "Get in touch with your tame informer in the Defense Department and find out if Creaghmiller is turning in reports to anyone over there. Try and find out what's in them, and try to find out who he's *really* working for."

"You're thinking of Thurlow?" Jill asked. "I don't know if he'd put out *that* much effort to scuttle the project."

"Bullshit!" Hammer grumped. "It may not *be* any effort for him if he's already got Creaghmiller in his pocket. On the other hand, you don't want to start rattling Thurlow's cage until we know more. After all, Creaghmiller *may* only be a Russian spy."

After that remark, Jill couldn't feel tense any more. She laughed out loud, long and heartily.

Hammer smiled. He liked her laugh. "In the

meantime," he continued, "I'll tighten up on Mr. Creaghmiller. Whatever he types in there, he doesn't leave it in his office. Maybe he leaves it at home. I don't know. I'll have someone drop in when he's not around, and do some snooping."

"Snooping?"

"Sure. Nothing elaborate, you understand. Just the routine intense surveillance that's done periodically on people in sensitive jobs who have high security clearances." Colonel Hammer ticked them off on his fingers. "Put an automatic tap on his phone. Read his mail before it's delivered. Find out about his social life, if any. Keep a mileage log on his car to see if he goes very far away at any regular interval. Look over bank records. Maybe we'll have our master fire control computer make up a digital mosaic analysis on his shredded waste-paper—reconstruct it the way it was before he shredded it."

"That's monstrous," Jill snorted.

"Eh?" he said. "Of course it is. Is the brassbound liberal upset about invasion of privacy?"

"You bet your time-in-grade I am!" Jill said.

"How is that?" Hammer asked, feigning curiosity. "Are you upset about invasion of privacy in general, or just when it's 'out there,' somewhere, and doesn't supply you personally or professionally with intelligence information? How about all of your 'friends' around Washington? Don't you use tidbits of information from them to keep competitive? Don't you advance your career with the intelligence data they furnish?"

"That's different!" she shouted, without thinking how ridiculous the words would sound when spoken. . . . *(Why am I on the defensive, all of a sudden? I'm supposed to be the one who has the bulge on* him.) . . .

"You know that waiter in the *La Châtelaine*," Hammer asked, "—in the Mayflower Hotel— where you used to meet Chelsey Quincannon all the time?"

Jill Kernan turned slightly pale.

"Well," Hammer continued, "his name is Bob Garvey. Good egg, old Bob. Used to be my supply sergeant in Nam. We keep in touch."

"Now, just a minute!" Jill bristled. "I haven't done anything out of line!"

"Nothing I could pin on you, you mean. I was hot about that little spy job Chelsey did for you. I was *really* hot when you railroaded me into this job, but I guess you know that. What you may not know is that Chelsey and I have been friends for years. I encouraged her to get a commission and endorsed her application for officer training. Anyway— Joe Stewart and I had you out of the running there for a while, but Chelsey helped you box me back in, and you got her a berth in Giant-Killer as payment for her help."

"Now, just a minute, Hammer. You make her sound like—"

"Sure I do," he replied. "It always does when you use the correct words—like buying, selling and trading—to describe the favors under the table. Well, you don't know it all, anyway. I'd have Chelsey's ass bounced right out of the Air Force— except for one thing."

"Oh, really! Why is that? Because she's a *wom-*

an? Because of *your sense of chivalry?* or, because you think she might be a *good lay,*'' Jill said sardonically.

''*No!* he thundered. ''*Because she's a top-notch pilot!*''

''Then that's why she got the job,'' Jill lashed back, ''not because she gave me necessary information! I needed something more than the press releases the military passes off as fitness reports. She believed enough in the project to want the best possible man for the job.

''You thought I was out of the running? Remember this, flyboy, I wanted you; I got you. And, if you don't perform, *I* will hand you your head in your hat!'' She turned toward the bar. ''Now, I think *I'll* have a drink.''

''Do you good,'' Hammer said mildly. ''Now that we've both flexed all our muscles, you think I can get the planes, or not?''

Jill dropped ice cubes into a glass—thoughtfully. *Plink. Plink. Plink.* ''Not for a while. If *you* can't get them, I can't either—*until* I can find out what's in the wind. Then, I can cut some corners. How long can you sit still and make do?''

''About a month.'' There was no hesitation in his voice. He had already worked out alternate operations plans. ''I can throw the load on Egghead Flight—Jill-Two—for a while. Jill-One is due for a rest, anyway, and we've *got* to tear into their planes and do some pretty heavy work on them. We'll be into the main tornado season before we know it. That means heavy flying requirements for everyone. Jill-Three is in training, but we won't be getting

them at McConnell soon enough to take any of the
pressure off this airplane problem.''

Jill chewed her lip and offered her hand. "Well,
Dan. Hang in there. I'll do the best I can at this end.
Shake on it?"

"Sure," he said, smiling. "Like it or not, it looks
like we're in bed together—uh—as far as Giant-
Killer is concerned."

Jill's ears reddened. She could feel them burning,
but was determined not to acknowledge it.

Hammer knew he should keep his mouth shut. but
he couldn't resist another sudden impulse. "By the
way, Ms. Brassbound Liberal . . . I've been thinking about you and our 'privacy' discussion. Is your
office bugged?"

"Of course not!"

"How do you know?"

"I have a man come in and sweep it once a week
for electronic devices."

"Does he change the tape on your machines at the
same time?" Hammer asked innocently.

"He—Get out of here, Hammer! You'll be hearing from me."

"Yeah," he said.

Chapter 10

During the taxi ride back to Andrews AFB, Colonel Daniel Hammer worked out in his mind the details of a security system—perfectly innocent and routine—which would deny Mr. Craven Creaghmiller the kind of free access to the planes of Operation Giant-Killer he had previously enjoyed. Creaghmiller would, of course, continue to compile information from the tornado-killing project, but his accumulation of data and conclusions would be carefully orchestrated by Hammer, through his crew chiefs and ground NCOs. Then, there was the switcheroo aspect. That would take some careful handling, but it wasn't all that complicated.

Jill Kernan had just roughed out a list of phone

calls, appointments-to-be-made, and completed a
critical path sheet for their organized accomplish-
ment. Some elements *had* to follow the aquisition
of other elements. Many though, would have to be
grabbed on the run.

"Yes. Mildred," she was saying into the intercom, coaching her receptionist, "and get Leon the
best way you can. That's right; rearrange my
schedule to fit his. . . . *(Dan Hammer isn't the
bossy egomaniac I thought he was . . .) . . .* I
know, Mildred, but make it for cocktails, luncheon,
breakfast—whatever can be put together right
away. . . . *(As a matter of fact, he's* entitled *to be
a pushy bastard, as long as he gets things done.)*
. . . Well, do the best you can. If anyone in the
Pentagon gets a hangnail, Leon knows about it
while the guy is still chewing on it. . . ." *(Stop
it! You're rationalizing Daniel Hammer's worst
traits! Well, so what? He's not a bad person, once
you begin to get to know him . . .) . . .*

In the Officers' Open Mess at Andrews AFB,
more complex conspiracies are hatched than are
little turtles after a turtle orgy.

Colonel Dan Hammer eyed Major General Joe
Stewart for a moment before he reacted to a particularly vitriolic remark the latter had just made about
a certain lady senator from California.

"Oh, I don't know about that, Joe," he said.
"She's not so bad; once you kind of get to know
her."

"All right, Dan. Let's not get a can of worms
opened up about that. I suppose it all depends on

whose ox is getting gored, anyway. Besides, I've
let you talk me into a 'severe reprimand' level plot
to help you out, here, so don't get me all stirred up,
or I may back out and cut your throat, just for the
sake of doing you a mean one.''

Hammer smiled lopsidedly. ''What are friends
for, Joe? It won't come back on you, anyway. I just
need you to talk to 'Old Storm Trooper.' Not that I
don't know him well enough, myself, but it would
be a little brash for me to whip such a plot onto a
flag-rank officer. Coming from one of his peers,
though, it will seem reasonable. I don't think we'll
have to do this sort of thing for more than a few
months, anyway. When Operation Giant-Killer
proves up, we'll get more money and better aircraft.
Very soon I'm going to have major aircraft components and systems that aren't safe to repair, and I
can't legally get spares. If Old Storm Trooper
agrees, I'll just D-X the bad material and he can bury
it in his regular report-of-survey on turned-in Phantoms that they scrap through his Logistics Command
at Wright-Patterson.''

''Old Storm Trooper'' was an in-service
monicker of respectful admiration for Lieutenant
General Axel T. Johnsen, Jr. It was never used to
his face, although he knew of its general application
to him. In fact, he took a good deal of secret pride
in it.

General Johnsen was a direct and pragmatic fellow.

One morning he had been sitting in his office,
dictating correspondence of the routine sort that requires response from the base commander of a

military installation. He had become increasingly irritated by the noise of a chainsaw being wielded by a civilian contractor in a nearby grove of trees.

Finally, General Johnsen had fetched his personal .45 automatic from the drawer of his desk, tucked it in his belt, and walked out of his headquarters. Upon arriving at the grove of trees, he ambled up to the man with the chainsaw and made some genial smalltalk, which culminated in a direct question as to the value of the man's chainsaw. Informed that its cost was a little under one hundred forty dollars, General Johnsen expressed approval, dug into his pocket—he always maintained a gambler's-size roll of ready cash—and handed the civilian one hundred forty dollars. He nodded affirmatively to the man's question of whether purchase was indicated by the action.

To the stammered inquiry of why, he only motioned the civilian to stand out of the way. Then, he drew the service automatic from his belt and emptied seven shots into the helpless machine. "Don't ever cut my goddamned trees," he said, "and, don't make noise outside my goddamned office."

He walked back to his office and ordered a guard put on the grove of trees.

It is not surprising that such a man would be willing to allow Colonel Hammer to circumvent normal requisition regulations in the smooth manner Hammer had so carefully formulated.

Hammer would cull out unsafe aircraft components from the planes of Operation Giant-Killer. He would transfer ownership of these on a direct exchange basis—D-X them, as they said in the trade—with identical plane components owned by Old Storm Trooper's Air Force Logistics Command. No one would sign for anything. There would be no paperwork—only an occasional tinkering with a serial number. Nothing would ever appear in the records as a supply action.

You got a shaky turbine? Switch it with the one in another aircraft that is to be turned in because of unserviceable hydraulics. It was the common and oft-practiced version of the "new lamps for old" tactic in the story of Aladdin. It cost the taxpayers nothing. It kept Hammer under budget and the planes in the air.

There was more than one way to skin a senator.

From that point on, Creaghmiller's readings would be taken with the "assistance" of an officer from Investigation, masquerading as the "engineering liason officer." Creaghmiller would get the data he sought so passionately. He would get what Hammer *wanted* him to get.

The fourth opportunity for a tornado kill took the form of a small but evil-looking twister near Dodge City.

Hammer curbed an itch to lead the mission himself. He assigned the mission to Egghead Flight, but covered his bet by assigning Lt. Peter Selby to lead. He wanted to bolster Jill-Two's first mission with his most experienced pilot out in front.

Everything went smoothly on the scramble and chase phases of the mission. Textbook perfection made Dan Hammer uneasy. He neither liked nor

trusted the easy perfection of "school solutions."
In real life they could turn treacherous.

Selby began his bomb run at five hundred ninety
knots. He flashed across the I.P. and punched the
autopilot for ATTACK. Nothing happened. In the
two seconds it took him to react, recognize the trouble, and override the controls, the target was a third
of a mile closer.

"Abort! Abort!" screamed Selby, working the
controls to recover his plane. "Egghead-Leader
here! Abort! Abort! New approach!"

He threw the Phantom into a hard 5g bank to
starboard, pulling to one side of the tornado in a
tight turn and aiming to lay up for a second pass as
soon as the other two planes had sheared after him.

The turbulence had increased greatly while Selby
reacted and attempted to recover. In the violent air
of the storm, the screaming F-4J hit an eddy-gust
going the other direction. The effect was much the
same as flying into a stone wall at Mach 1. The
Phantom folded her wings like a grotesquely stricken
bird for just a second, before they ripped completely
free of the fuselage.

Selby had time to radio "Mayday! Mayday!" as
he savagely punched the ejection button.

His Skysail chute blossomed in the tornado's
wake at fourteen hundred feet, going up instead of
down. Selby was helpless. He had no way to control the parachute, and he knew it. He nerved up for
a wild ride, but doubted that he had a chance of
surviving.

The draft rushing into the writhing force of the
vortex a half-mile away whipped his parachute aloft

and carried him in a narrowing helix that drew toward the vertical wall of the funnel cloud. As he swung in close, midway between earth and overcast, the tornado's howling wind snatched his chute horizontal. The acceleration was almost beyond endurance. Selby estimated the g-force and probability of blacking out. Centrifugal force pulled the muscles in his face out of shape as his bow-taut chute dragged him through a one hundred eighty-degree turn around the vortex. His head swam and a giant hand squeezed steadily against his chest, threatening to snap his ribs to splinters. Terrifying in its vast nearness, the rushing roar of the whirlwind enveloped him.

His body mass, swinging out from the focus of the vortex like a horizontal pendulum, forced the chute to collapse. Selby was hurled away from the center of the storm for the time it took his canopy to reinflate. Once again, the updraft snatched and held him. The wild wind carried him higher each time it dragged him along that agonizing spiral.

Dazed and sagging in his harness, Selby disappeared into the boiling clouds.

Chapter 11

"Just how high it carried him or how far he traveled before he died is not certain." A solemn Vern Graham was addressing the hastily formed Special Investigating Committee led by Senator Sam Thurlow.

"As you know," Graham continued, "Selby's body was never recovered. Even his parachute disappeared without a trace. We suspect that he was lifted to a very high altitude and most probably died of anoxia. Even at a lower altitude, in those clouds he could have frozen to death within a period of only minutes."

Graham paused, "I counted Selby as my good friend. This regrettable incident must never be repeated. I blame myself, as much as anyone. I was too anxious. If I had refused to accept the overaged and vulnerable equipment he was using, he might have survived.''

''Come, come, Dr. Graham,'' Senator Thurlow said expansively. ''We are all aware, as I'm sure you are, that many things could have contributed to this tragic disaster. Things other than simply blaming the whistle when no tune comes out of it.''

Graham drew himself together. He thought Thurlow had just insulted him, but it had been done in such a congenial and comradely fashion that he really couldn't be sure. He adjusted his glasses. ''Examination of the wreckage of Selby's plane supports the analysis readouts of the radar records, *and* the CompAn Update from the direction computers. There is no doubt whatever that the autopilot failed to respond as Selby released control of the aircraft to it. The onboard computer was new equipment. Its reliability has been established beyond any doubt whatsoever.''

Graham stared hard at Thurlow. ''This tragic loss must not blind us, Senator, to what has already been proven. Tornadoes *can be killed!* If no new obstacles are placed in our path, we will complete the test program as planned. We should not let the death of a fine young man— '' Graham had to stop for a second. ''Lives and property can be *saved!* Only recently we witnessed a demonstration, followed swiftly by another, of what the future can bring. We *cannot* abandon this program. We first owed it to the American people to *try*. Now, we owe it to Peter Selby to go forward . . . Thank you . . . " Dr. Graham slowly sat down in his chair, exhausted.

Senator Jill Kernan was the first to get the floor, and she jumped in with both feet. "May I add, gentlemen, that by carrying on with this worthy task, this enormous obligation which we have the power to fulfill, we can guarantee that Peter Selby did not die in vain. We simply cannot discard a program we now know can succeed."

"Thank you, Senator Kernan," Thurlow rumbled. He was looking even more dour than was his custom. "I'm appreciative of the sincerity of your sentiments and the high humanitarianism of your motives," he said in funereal tones. "The fact remains that to this date your tornado-killing program has enjoyed only fifty-percent effectiveness, and has been—" Thurlow cleared his throat huskily. "—very costly. What assurances can *now* be given that other brave pilots will not follow young Lieutenant Selby into the Shades of Death—to no avail? *I* cannot, in all good conscience, lend support to a proposal to continue this hazardous and ill-starred project."

Jill took a deep breath and faced Senator Thurlow squarely. "Defective equipment, aircraft unable to stand up to the strain of repeated tornado-killing, comes *directly* from false economies forced on the project at its inception. Everyone in this room is aware of the source of that economy policy. Let your good conscience consider *that*, Senator Thurlow."

Before Thurlow could counterattack, she went on. "Defense Department records show that both Dr. Graham and Colonel Hammer repeatedly filed requests for better equipment, a larger maintenance budget. They both acted in awareness and anticipation of the problems that later arose. Their requests were shuffled around to aircraft manufacturers and civilian contractors, where executives *pooh-poohed* them, fearing a slur on companies or products. Defense sat on its hands and did *nothing*. My own memos to Defense on this subject were pigeonholed into a 'study file.' A *study file!* The time for study was when we could have heard Lieutenant Selby's *testimony*, not his eulogies. *That* was the time to get off the dime, gentlemen. We stand here in shame today, *all of us!* The Senate, the House, the Defense Department, and those of us in this room have taken the trust of our office and the enemy we face so lightly that we have sat idly by and traded a young man's life *for false economies*.

"Personally, I am *ashamed* that I knuckled under to such shabby bargaining. If *I*, with the support of a few colleagues, had howled bloody murder as soon as the facts were presented by Colonel Hammer and Dr. Graham, Peter Selby might still be alive.

"The die is cast, gentlemen. No more back-room political deals. I intend to honor the commitments I have already made, but there will be no new compromises. While breath remains in my body, Operation Giant-Killer will not be prevented from proving that its merciful goal *can* be realized."

The die *was* cast. The fate of Giant-Killer depended on a showdown between animated young Senator Jill Kernan and shaggy old Senator Sam Thurlow.

The matter had gone too far now to be solved without blood. Jill had lost her temper. Thurlow had found it, but didn't want it. Earlier, Jill had made a deal with Thurlow. Thurlow would vote for Giant-Killer as a federal program if Kernan would shut down her news and publicity machinery on the subject. Both had agreed not to comment publicly on the Giant-Killer program. When Jill had learned that the project had been short-changed on the equipment it needed to do its job, she had become angry and suspicious. When Selby died, Jill Kernan realized that she had been sucked in—that Thurlow *intended* Giant-Killer to fail, so he could later have his own way with the program's concept. That made Jill furious. She fired up an oratorical blow-torch to force the matter into the open. She intended to push the entire affair into a public hearing, hopefully before the full Armed Forces Committees of the Congress.

Those who reclined at very lofty altitudes on the slopes of political Olympus were beginning to stir, beginning to take an interest in this "little experimental program" which was churning up such a tempest.

That was what Jill wanted. She wanted the news media to start digging. She wanted the President, if possible, to get interested enough to study the file on Operation Giant-Killer.

The joint committee hearing functioned under the chairmanship of the floor leader and the senior member of the Senate—the Honorable Erwin Culpepper Pogue.

Senator Pogue rapped the gavel and turned loose

the dogs of politics on the legislative floor of the enormous caucus room where the hearing was to be held. Sitting still as a stone, his hearing aid volume carefully modulated, Senator Pogue gave not one indication that he was listening to the tempest of debate. He was quietly leafing through a book, pausing occasionally for periods of apparently deep thought.

" . . . and let the record show," Senator Thurlow rhapsodized as he paced solemnly back and forth before the committee table, piercing his colleagues with a statesmanly gaze, "that, while the original proposals for this program were in the Senate committee, I held the unenviable position of trying to act as a balance wheel—a steadying influence to prevent this sort of ill-advised rushing forward before all the facts were in. I was willing to be branded as obdurate, then. And, I tell you now, ladies and gentlemen, I would cheerfully endure such vilification a thousand times if it would prevent the dealings which brought about the death of young Lieutenant Peter Selby.

"In the action before this body, the question is put—and I am proud to be a co-author of the joint resolution—that we do not simply throw away the funds already spent, the aircraft modification, the ordnance, the four-million dollar airplane which took Selby to his death," Thurlow paused dramatically and spun on his heel, giving time for the *four million dollars* to sink into the minds of the press gallery, "and the untimely loss of a brilliant young officer. This resolution pleads for time to acquire the knowledge we need."

The question before the committee was that of disbanding Operation Giant-Killer, with the proviso that a study commission be appointed to sift and sort the available information, evaluate the total picture of tornado damage, the possibilities and alternatives for abatement, and on and on. When a report was finally to be given, then recommendations might be made to reinstate the program and revive Operation Giant-Killer. Maybe. It could easily take a couple of years to prepare the report.

While Senator Thurlow spoke, Senator Kernan was thinking, *You son-of-a-bitch. You can see that the program is sound as it stands. Selfish you may be, but you're not stupid. Give Giant-Killer a black eye, now. Salt it away on the shelf and urge the caution of "Study." When the time comes, after you've milked the publicity out of killing it off, you can bring it back as your own idea—preferably during an election year—and milk it some more. Show the yokels how brilliant you are. Show us the right way to do this. Fuck you, Thurlow. I'll see your ass busted for this if it's the last thing I ever do.*

Jake Tannenbaum was introducing an amended resolution to permit continued operation of the Giant-Killer program.

"Study, if study will serve the good of the people." He tugged at his vest. "The good of the people is what we are sworn to uphold.

"My worthy colleague, Senator Thurlow, has always stood like a lion at the gates of the public treasury, and fought for the good of the people of this land—without regard for his own gain, letting the chips fall where they might. And, such a courageous man can certainly admit, from his own background—a background that was not lacking in the training and fostering of Christian ideals of charity for and love of neighbor—that the lion and the lamb may certainly repose together and partake of nourishment under a single roof. Study, if study will serve the good of the people. Study begets scholarship. *Need* begets action. And, if scholarship is the lamb, then action must be the lion.

"The very nature of knowledge is study, ladies and gentlemen, and I strongly agree that there must be continuing study of Operation Giant-Killer. But, surely there is more knowledge to be gained from the study of something that is alive and working to fulfill its goal than can possibly be gleaned from a pile of dusty records—the static legacy of a thing that is dead, a thing that has been killed because it did not perform one hundred percent perfect, *letter-perfect*. What man among us could weigh his own continuing life against this perfection? I call to mind, ladies and gentlemen, that in the ancient and bewhiskered joke about the farmer, his mule, and his young wife, *that* most intemperate of men allowed even his mule *three* mistakes before shooting it dead.

"When I was a youngster on the streets of Brooklyn, I can remember that my mother was possessed of a sufficiently vast store of homespun wisdom that she could call to mind some proverb, some aphorism, some allegory, some analog of philosophy—often an entire anthology of them bearing on any given occurrence—so as to sound as though she had instantly coined the example for the purpose of explaining the situation immediately at hand.''

Senator Tannenbaum hooked his thumbs in his vest pockets and peered over his glasses. ''One day, my mother, together with Mrs. Ginsberg the neighbor lady, is getting ready potatoes for potato salad—yes? As they are washing these potatoes and Mrs. Ginsberg is boiling the eggs for the potato salad, my mother comes across a potato which is having a very strange appearance. It is, this strange potato, all bloated-looking, much like you would expect a potato with cancer to look if you are imagining a potato with cancer and how it might look.

''My mother holds up the potato to Mrs Ginsberg and says, 'Sarah! Look at this potato! I never saw such a potato.' 'Neither have I,' says Mrs. Ginsberg. 'Do you think it's all right to eat?' my mother asks. Mrs. Ginsberg, a very pessimistic lady, says, 'Why take a chance, Mrs. Tannenbaum? Put the potato aside. Take it back to the merchant, next time you go to the store, and insist that he should replace it.'

''My mother thinks about this idea for a moment, and then she decides that satisfying her own curiosity about this strange potato is more important than the potato itself, which cannot be worth more than a few cents. My mother, you should understand, is a lady who is convinced about the reality of such things as finding stolen jewels baked into a loaf of bread, discovering a pearl necklace in the gizzard of a chicken, a gold watch in a goose egg, and many other such unlikely things that are dreamed about by

people in something less than elegant financial circumstances.

"Well, what do you think? Do you think my
mother cut open this potato and found a diamond
ring inside? Yes?" Jake Tannenbaum shook his
head slowly from side to side. He fished around in
his vest pocket and took hold of something, but did
not show it, drawing it out of the pocket as he
spoke. "Certainly not. But, there was—and we
must all admit that it is at least a little unusual—a
silver dollar *inside* this strange potato." He held up a
large coin for everyone in the room to observe, for
the newsmen to photograph, and for the television
cameras to record. He pointed to it with his other
hand. "This self-same *silver dollar*, ladies and gentlemen, *was inside that bloated and funny-looking
potato!*

"When the potato field had been planted, out on
Long Island, or in New Jersey, or God-knows-
where, someone had dropped a silver dollar in the
potato field. Maybe he had a hole in his pocket, or
was careless. Who knows? And, a potato—a
potato, ladies and gentlemen—grew around this
silver dollar. Now, I should point out, despite my
own youthful appearance, that those were the days
when a dollar was a *dollar*. A man could eat lunch
for a week on a dollar, and as for potatoes—well, a
dollar would buy more potatoes than the average
man could carry.

"My respected colleague, Senator Thurlow,
wants us to take our potato back to the storekeeper.
'This potato looks a little strange,' he says. 'Let's
play it safe with this strange potato,' he says.

"While we are studying this potato—this anti-tornado program—and while we are discussing whose fault it might be that this potato has a strange appearance, we stand in danger of *losing* the object of our concern and interest—*the good of the people*. Ladies and gentlemen, *let's not lose track of the potato until we find out what's inside it!*"

Chapter 12

God Almighty! thought Vernon Graham. *Once these guys get the floor, they hang on as though they expected to be struck mute the moment they yield back to the Chair. This mumbo-jumbo is taking us nowhere. Last night at dinner, Jake talked like there was nothing in the world he would like better than to take a shotgun and pump Sam Thurlow full of buckshot. Today, it's my worthy this and my honored that. Goose shit! And, here's Mrs. Graham's innocent son, caught square in the middle of these blithering bastards . . . Stranglehold on my budget by a bunch of fat shysters who don't know centigrade from centigram. My project means nothing to the posturing sons-o'-bitches.*

And glancing over at Dan Hammer, *then there's the Prussian monster . . . No, that's unkind. Still, I can't help thinking that while he's talking about killing tornadoes, he's thinking about some future point when the same techniques can be used to dump napalm on farmers with better target area control than we currently enjoy.*

Damn it! Damn it! Damn it! They're trying to dismember my experiment before it's proved. They're tearing my work to pieces, and I feel so damned helpless!

Jake Tannenbaum was concluding his amendment proposal. '' . . . to maintain a level of operation that will utilize the equipment already at hand, and the personnel already trained. Operation Giant-Killer is too important—dare I say it?—too relevant to the immediate needs of the American people. To just scrap it, to shunt it aside, like —''

''Will the gentleman from New York yield to a point of personal privilege?''Senator Thurlow interrupted.

''The *Senior Senator from the State of New York,*'' Tannenbaum said evenly, ''will *consider* yielding to such a point if he is advised beforehand of its nature and believes it so important that it truly cannot accomodate waiting on the completion of his remarks.''

''It has to do,'' Thurlow said, ''with the improper nature of this amendment's introduction. I would, if allowed the point, call upon the Chairman of the Rules Committee to verify the cogency of the point. It involves precedence under Senate Rule number—''

"Not required," Tannenbaum snapped back. "Standing rules under immediate consideration apply by prior consent and agreement to the introduction of the joint resolution here under consideration. I will yield the floor directly *after* I have concluded, but predjudicial . . . "

Remarks! Remarks! Colonel Daniel Hammer was thinking obscene thoughts about politicians in general. *You lousy sons-o'-bitches have the fucking gall to talk about Selby. Jerk a tear or two from the gallery. If he were here he'd spit in your sanctimonious goddam eye. And kick you in the balls every time you mealy-mouth another goddam "in vain." "Shall not have died in vain." Is there any other way to die? Let's ask the guy who gets dead. You fuckers think every time you wrap a flag around a coffin you can cover your own ass with it.*

One guy gets cashed in because he was flying junk, and the politicians that forced him to fly junk all get in line to rot their shoes with crocodile tears about what a fine fellow he was, what a shame it had to happen, what a waste of the flower of America's brave young men. Horse shit! Selby knew he was flying junk. I knew he was flying junk. But could we get it fixed up straight? Not while we had to elbow somebody else away from the trough! Now he's dead and everybody is scared to death they might get the blame—when they know damned well they deserve the blame.

Men get blown away in combat for the same reasons and nobody turns a hair. Chalk it off to enemy action and forget it. We know it's because some civilian contractor skimmed a little too much, employed a little too much "fabrication economy," greased a few too many palms, lined a few too many pockets. We know inspectors don't always do their job, can be persuaded to look the other way. A few can be just plain bought. But none of those guys are ever around when some poor bastard's guns jam, or his flaps jam, or his rudder jams, or his goddam plane starts to break up in a dive. We're good enough to fly and die in junk, but when we get up on our hind legs and call *it junk, they say we're alibiing for pilot error to cover for each other. If you cocksucking politicians took all your honesty, put it together, and stuck it in my ear, there would still be room for three caraway seeds and a drill sergeant's heart.*

Why *do we go out and fight for people like that?* Hammer had to think hard for an answer, and he still wasn't satisfied with it. *Somebody has to go out and fight for them.*

He fell into just cussing for the general good of his soul.

Jake Tannenbaum had introduced his rider to the joint resolution, and the debate was wrangling. Thurlow had gotten the floor, yielded it to one of his cronies, who had yielded it to another crony, who had yielded back to Thurlow.

"And what are we to gain from such an enterprise?" Thurlow asked expansively. He was wound up into his best spellbinder's form by now. "Ill-starred grandstanding by those so accustomed to dealing in death, so hardened to the shameful waste of the flower of America's brave young men, that they deal in 'acceptable casualty levels,' 'normal troop wastage,' and 'enemy body count.' That's the administrative posture military commanders are used to. Have we—I ask you, ladies and gentlemen—placed ourselves in a frame of mind that is conducive to a productive program here, or have we allowed ourselves to be bamboozled—yes, I said *bamboozled!*—into providing a circus arena—a cruel coliseum—for peacetime heroics by military adventurers?''

Before Thurlow had completed the sentence, Dan Hammer was on his feet and moving toward the committee table.

Jill's heart leaped into the back of her throat when she saw him. She had no idea what he was up to, but there was no way to stop him.

"Senator Thurlow!" Dan Hammer shouted as he reached the open space which separated the seats from the committee table and the congressmen, officers, attorneys, and clerks. "*Somebody* has got to protest your slanders. If there is no one on this committee, no one in the Congress, no one in this room who will—then *I* will have to!''

Thurlow spun toward Senator Pogue. "*Point of order!*" he thundered. "This officer is out of order and acting in contempt of this body!''

Senator Pogue looked up from his book. "And who might this person be?" he asked, although he knew Dan Hammer perfectly well.

"He is the military—" Thurlow began.

"Shush up," cautioned Senator Pogue. "Identify yourself, young man.''

"Sir! Colonel Daniel W. Hammer, United States

Air Force, commanding the 918th test squadron."

Pogue nodded. "Stationed at McConnell AFB?" he asked, "And assigned to the anti-tornado project known as Operation Giant-Killer?"

"Yes, sir," Hammer replied, slightly bewildered.

"Let the record so show," Pogue said dryly.

"I most vigorously *protest* this disruption," Thurlow trumpeted, "and herewith request the Chairman of this body to order the sergeant-at-arms to *remove* Colonel Hammer from these chambers."

Pogue rapped the gavel. Once. Twice. The hum of conversation on the floor subsided. "If we throw Colonel Hammer out, we won't hear what he has to say. Somethin' *is* weighin' mighty heavy on his mind."

"I *protest*," Senator Thurlow repeated. "I will *not* yield the floor to this highly irregular display of theatrics, so obviously staged to—"

Senator Pogue rapped the gavel once more. "Shut up, Sam," he said. "The Chair invokes personal privilege and directs that Colonel Hammer's statement be included in the record by the clerk, but that it is not to be considered as a part of the debate on the question before the joint committee. His remarks shall not exceed five minutes. So ordered."

Thurlow took a step forward, but Senator Pogue held up his gavel in a rather threatening manner.

Senator Pogue blinked his watery eyes. For a second he looked even more senile than usual. Then, he leaned forward and eyed Dan Hammer closely. "Proceed, young man," he said, and returned to perusing his book.

Daniel Hammer swept the room with his gaze, trying to look into the secret hearts of the congressmen there, knowing he would be a damned fool to look for help, and trying to think of a way to say what he wanted to say so that it would touch them and be understandable to them.

This is insane, Hammer thought. *You sure stuck your prick in the pickle-slicer, Hammer. It doesn't seem like such a good idea now, but you've got to go ahead. You let old Thurlow goad you into losing your temper—somewhat less than productive or intelligent. He called you out into the street and you came running like a dumb green kid.*

Well, get going, damn it.

"Times change, attitudes change, technology changes, and the knowledge that man possesses moves forward. The more humanity knows, the more it can learn. Such is the *nature* of progress— from fire to the wheel to iron; to steam, and on through the engines of man to the jet plane and the vessels that are carrying men on the new seas of space to other planets.

"But, there are some things that never change. In ancient times, Roman soldiers plagued the armorer with gripes that the pommel sat too loosely on the tang if a sword was made a certain way. They complained about the lousy leather covering the handholds on the average issue shield. The basic glue of human nature which holds civilization together never changes. Soldiers don't become something else—they are already soldiers. The cut and the color of the uniforms has changed. The nature of the weapons men hurl at each other has changed. But the soldier under that skin of technology is the same now as he was at the dawn of time.

"And, he considers that he has a soldierly privilege to complain about something which strikes him as deficient. The right to gripe is the mark of the military trade. But why should it be? What is so different about *my* profession, that a constant stream of bitching and bellyaching is still considered to be a symptom of a healthy happy soldier?

"It is a safety valve, ladies and gentlemen. It releases the pressure of this occupation's stress. No matter how sublimely peaceful the state of the world may be, anyone wearing a uniform knows that serenity can change in the wink of an eye. And when it does, he will be called to put his living body on the line to protect his employers, the people of the country he serves.

"He knows during peacetime that his existence is a kind of anachronism to those employers. Having soldiers around when there is no war is a vague sort of national embarrassment. Peacetime military forces are resented, as a general rule, and the public rationale for their existence is often unconvincing. It usually comes down to begrudging the money spent on those military forces.

"Operation Giant-Killer really has two purposes. The first, of course, is to kill tornadoes. Sounds very simple when you just come out and say it. Killing tornadoes. In fact, though, we have taken a new step down a fresh road to declare war on one of our oldest and most formidable natural enemies. The second purpose is to maintain a level of profi-

ciency in our military pilots which will keep them
combat-ready. This last we must do in any case if
those planes and pilots are to be of any service to us
when—and if—we should need them for national
defense. Operation Giant-Killer blends these factors together. It has the capability of removing
some of that national embarrassment about a nation
at peace maintaining a strong military force.

"Until we need them, we, a democratic and free
nation, must keep the dogs of war chained up some
way. We must have them available. There are still
nations on this planet who only understand the
quick availability of raw force as the finest expression of another nation's strength. But we are a
peace-loving people and rather shy about making
show of our armed readiness. We want to be *ready*
for a fight without appearing to desire it.

"Operation Giant-Killer puts the dogs of war in a
role that is hard for the civilian to understand. The
civilian rarely understands the military men he
pays wages to protect him and his peace of mind.
The civilian often finds it difficult to tell when
something is dead and when it is merely taking a
short nap. The confusion about the part played by
the dogs of war in Operation Giant-Killer should
not, then, be surprising to anyone.

"And yet, it seems to be constantly surprising to
everyone."

Hammer was beginning to loosen up. He had the
attention of everyone in the room, and he thought
he was swaying them to the idea—novel for most
legislators—that there could be such a thing as a
career officer who was literate, reasonable, articu-

late, and interested in communicating with them. Only Senator Thurlow was fidgeting and whispering to those seated around him. Hammer wanted to step up and belt him one.

"The business of the soldier, ladies and gentlemen," Hammer continued, "is life. That may seem contradictory. How can a trade that deals in handing out death possibly concern itself with the saving of life? I think it is only fair to point out that our job is to keep peace, not make war. We are called in only after the civilian statesmen and lawmakers have decided to fight. No one despises war more than the regular soldier. He *knows* there is no glory in it, no solution from it. For him and for his comrades there is only blood and death in it.

"What Senator Thurlow says is correct as far as it goes, but he does not understand what he is saying. It is perfectly true that those in my profession are hardened to death and destruction and killing. But it is no more our *business* than it is the *business* of the surgeon to cut human flesh and watch the blood flow from the wound. His job is to heal the body; our job is to heal society. The difference is this; you people never call *us* in until the body of society appears to be in a terminal condition. It is unfortunate, then, but perhaps necessary, and certainly understandable, that both the surgeon and the soldier sometimes lose their patients.

"We don't shy from doing our jobs. We expect to bet our lives on our organization, our discipline, and the equipment we use. But, it frightens and angers us for you to gamble with our lives seeking to save a few dollars, even a few *million* dollars.

When you people do that, you are in effect telling us that our lives aren't worth a damn, or that you simply don't understand the nature of our risk-taking. I don't know which surmise is the more appalling.

"Dr. Graham and I repeatedly begged the Defense Department for enough equipment to do the job. Someone thought we were empire-building, careless with the taxpayers' bucks, or just griping. The *real* cause of Peter Selby's death is the stupid lack of concern and refusal to listen by those who *had it in their power* to correct the faults in the program when those faults were repeatedly pointed out. Senator Thurlow thinks Selby died as a result of some kind of dashing recklessness on the part of 'military adventurers.' That's not so. It's true he could have refused to fly junk against tornadoes. He would have been completely within his rights and in accord with his oath of service. But Selby didn't do that. He continued to fly, as did every other pilot of mine, because he knew it was *more important to get the job done*."

Senator Thurlow was waving at the clerk and pointing to his own watch.

Hammer turned to face him. "I am well aware, Senator Thurlow, that the time so courteously allotted to me by Senator Pogue is nearly over, and I shall complete my remarks as speedily as I can.

"Peter Selby didn't die for nothing. He proved two things. He, along with the rest of us in Operation Giant-Killer, laid down the foundation from which we can *prove* the practicality of killing tor-

nadoes with military aircraft. Sadly, he also proved
that we must have a tougher airplane than the Phantom II in order to get the job done safely.

"That, essentially, is why I felt I had to speak up.
When you slander our profession, sir, you slander
Peter Selby. You slander me. And you slander every
one of us who routinely risks his or her life for your
benefit.

"I realize it must sound a little ponderous to call
the military trade a life and death situation during
peace time. But, when it's time to *do* the job, that's
what it comes down to. We know that; you should
know it, but sometimes don't. I wish that I could
stand here today and tell you for sure that if you
give us what Dr. Graham and I ask for, no more
Giant-Killer pilots will die. I can't. I'd be a fool to
even suggest it.

"The Apollo program had more fail-safe systems
in it than any flying job ever attempted and still it
cost lives. The astronauts *knew* that some of them
would die. Still, they went ahead and got the job
done. I don't mean to equate the importance of
Giant-Killer with the Apollo Program. What I *do*
mean is this: I can't give you inflexible assurances,
because in attaining goals *men do die*.

"Ladies and gentlemen, I beg you not to throw
Operation Giant-Killer aside. It is a good program,
aimed at accomplishing a worthwhile goal that will
save life while it helps us keep the peace."

Hammer eyed his adversary. "If that made me a
'military adventurer,' Senator Thurlow, then I
would tell you to go straight to hell. Since I am not,
I needn't say that."

Dan Hammer turned to look over the room. "Thank you," he said, then turned and walked back up the aisle.

There was a second's silence, heavy with tension, like the still air before a thunderstorm. Then, Jill Kernan began to clap—all alone for several seconds—gradually joined by her fellow congressmen until most of them were on their feet applauding thunderously.

Sam Thurlow was on his feet too, but he was shouting at Senator Pogue to call for order and give him the floor.

Senator Pogue gazed over the legislators and spectators and let them applaud for several seconds. Then, he bent his microphone down close to the table, so that the rap of his gavel cracked through the hall like a pistol shot.

In the sudden silence that followed, the microphone creaked loudly as Pogue returned it to position.

"Point of order! Point of order!" Thurlow said noisily. "Colonel Hammer has told a member of the United States Senate to go to hell! I *protest* this abuse, and appeal to the Chair that his remarks be stricken from the record as a result of such an impudent insult to a member of this body!"

Thurlow paused for the reaction from the Chair.

Senator Pogue sighed and closed his book loudly. "Colonel Hammer's remarks will stand, since they were brought to the floor and introduced by call for personal privilege of the presiding officer. As to the honorable Senator's complaint and appeal to the Chair," He tapped the book with his index finger. "I've been looking at the Rules, Sam. You don't have to go."

After the general laughter had died away, and a somewhat subdued Senator Thurlow had returned to his seat, Senator Pogue blinked his watery eyes and allowed a wan smile to play over his face. He made a minute adjustment of his hearing aid. "The Chair will entertain a motion that we 'journ fo'r lunch," he said.

Chapter 13

Humiliation didn't take all the wind out of Thurlow's sails. He was elegantly proficient at infighting. Jake Tannenbaum's amendment to retain Giant-Killer as an active program during study by an appointed commission failed by a narrow margin.

The allocated funds in the Defense Department would be impounded for a length of time not specified more closely than "until a commission appointed on joint-preferential bases has completed a thorough study." That meant everyone would get to pick two members of the commission—Defense, Dr. Graham, Colonel Hammer, the Senate Armed Services Committee, the President, et cetera. The commission would function as a committee to gather information, sift data, and finally make some recommendations.

It was a dead cinch that at least a year would pass before anything emerged. During that year, another four hundred million dollars in property would be destroyed by tornadoes. Several thousand human beings would be injured, and something on the order of four or five hundred more citizens would die.

"Study!" exploded Dan Hammer. "The bastards want to study us to death!" He angrily bounced up from the couch in Jill Kernan's office. "It would be by-god different if we had a problem with no solution. God damn it, this is right in front of us! These bastards want to keep us from proving Vern Graham's theories with hard facts.

"Sons-o'-bitches," he muttered as he opened the panel to Jill's office bar. He ran his hand through his salt-and-pepper hair and surveyed the lighted array of clean glassware in the wall cabinet. "Goddam dog-humping politician sons-o'-bitches." He had to stoop his tall frame to look inside the cabinet, installed at a counter-height convenient for Jill. "Don't bend over, soldier-boy. In the U.S. of A. Congress they play drop-the-soap with Ivory Flakes." He whistled tunelessly through his teeth. "And, the politicians are the flakes." He laughed with a short, hard, barking sound. "Fucking shysters."

"Oh shut up, Dan," Jill said. "I'm a politician, too, you know, a shyster. You've got the Goddamnedest string of barrack-talk in you for a man who was so damned eloquent this morning.''

"Comes from my common background, my dear. When I was an enlisted-type NCO I was *really* a profane old bastard.''

Jill was starting to crack at the seams a little. "Well,'' she said, with a slight quaver in her voice, "do you think I'm a politician son-of-a-bitch, too? Because they're going to shut down Giant-Killer?''

Hammer set down the glass and turned quickly, only to find that Jill had walked up close behind him. He planted a large and expansively wet kiss on her mouth. "No, my dear, I do not. You admit you're a politician. Those fuckers think they're statesmen. *That* makes them dangerous. I automatically dis-include you from any snotty appellations I apply to your — ugh — colleagues.'' He kissed her again, before she could recover from the first one, then spun on his heel to continue preparing his drink.

"Don't go too heavy on the righteous wrath number,'' she said evenly. "You had them all, more or less, eating out of your hand in there. If you had been able to curb your male-ego-bull-apes-slugging-it-out-on-the-field-of-honor impulse to get old Thundercheeks Thurlow all stirred up, things might have skated through. God damn it, Dan! You can't tell a senator to go to hell "like he was some enlisted man who rubbed you the wrong way before breakfast. And you *sure* as hell can't do it on his own territory, in front of all his pals, cronies, and henchmen.''

"Crap!'' Hammer growled moodily. "I didn't

exactly *tell* him to go to hell. Just told him I would if I were what he had called *me*." Hammer laughed, low and in the back of his throat, like a Borgia plotting some minor throat-cutting.

"Well, I'm glad *your* ribs are tickled!" Jill's voice was rising. "Jake Tannenbaum's amendment stood a good chance of sliding through on the coat-tails of the study resolution. It was a good compromise, and didn't involve anyone losing face. *But, no!* You had to toss a couple of raw eggs on old Thurlow's vest. He *couldn't* do anything but react, so he got it all together before the vote came down— twisted some arms, called some favors, made some deals. You can bet this will be one time when the wheels of bureaucracy won't turn slowly. When Defense lays on that suspension order, it will be fired down to McConnell so fast it will make your thick, stubborn head swim."

Dan Hammer grunted assent, studying the ice cubes in his glass as though he expected to find the answer to his dilemma engraved on one of them.

Jill dabbed at her eyes with a tissue and then blew her nose loudly. "Well, don't just stand there, you big lunk! Fix me a drink, too."

"Mmmmmmmmmm," Hammer intoned, as he turned back to the bar. "Jill, " he began slowly, "you've got to get me an audience with the President."

She stared out the window for a long moment, while hope battled with common sense. "Bullshit! Go through channels, Hammer." She blew her nose again. "He's got a military advisor, you know. Some dowdy old general who invariably asks me to dance and then marches all over my feet.''

Colonel Hammer squinted at the wall and bared his teeth. "Yeah, I know," he said grudgingly, "but he never did like me very much. I know what *he'd* say if I asked to get into the oval office. No, that won't do. I think I could sell Giant-Killer to the President . . .''

"Hmph!" Jill muttered into the tissue. "You could sell contraceptives on the Vatican steps.''

"What?" Hammer asked.

"Nothing!" She blew her nose, again.

"I could sell Giant-Killer to the President if I could get about a half-hour alone with him—in some non-rigid setting, something besides a *vis-à-vis* meeting, with a desk between us—''

"And sell yourself to him, too," Jill said. *"Hah!"*

Hammer buffed his fingernails on the lapel of his uniform. "Why, shucks, ma'am—that done go without sayin'. Why, mah li'l ol' burgeois charm can wrap anyone 'round mah li'l ol' finger. Let's see now . . . I think it should be luncheon, or a brisk walk on the south lawn. Hey, how about—''

"Forget it, Dan," Jill said, rather snappishly. She took a big swig of her drink. "Boy, it's no accident that the trade slang for 'colonel' is 'bull.' You're *not* going to see the President. *I'm* not going to see the President. *None of us* are going to see the President. That's just the kind of shortcut Thurlow and his gang are waiting for us to try.''

"Oh," he said. "I hadn't thought about that.''

"Well, you haven't been fighting The Battle of Capitol Hill as long as I have. Protocol means everything at this point. We must not give old Thundercheeks any more ammunition. Certainly none that involves breach of administrative etiquette. Besides, there's the risk to be considered."

"What risk?" Hammer asked innocently.

"The President might make some slur on the military profession. You would then give him a sound ass-chewing and wave your fist in his face. The Secret Service would see it all and every one of us would land in the clink for conspiracy against the personal carcass of the Commander-in-Chief. No, thank you, Colonel Hammer, no more favors for me. You have put my tail in a crack quite enough for one day. Forget it."

"Well!" Hammer blustered. "You were by-god clapping louder than anyone else. I don't have all that much experience as a snake-oil peddler—a damned sight less than any given *senator*—but I thought it was a rather eloquent and moving speech, what with no notes, or anything."

Jill smiled and shook her head. "Oh, you great, loveable lump. Of course it was a moving speech. Of course it was great. *Except* for the part where you thumbed your nose at Sam Thurlow."

Hammer glowered. "I thought that part was nicely restrained. What I *wanted* to do was step up and punch the old bastard in the teeth."

"I know the feeling well," she said quickly, "but if I had punched old Thundercheeks every time I wanted to, he'd be on his seventh set of dentures and my right arm would be two inches shorter than it is."

"So," Hammer asked, "did you applaud just to make me feel good?"

"*Well,* I could hardly hiss and boo, could I? Seriously, Dan, it was a fine speech, and true. But, dammit!" Jill said exasperatedly, "don't they teach you lifers—I mean, career officers—*anything* about getting along with civilians? Especially civilian officials—most of whom don't know a damned thing about the aggravations *you* have to put up with every day? Isn't there a—a—some extension course in how to not rub politicians the wrong way?"

Hammer grunted and shrugged. "Yeah, We had something like that in staff college. Called—lemmee see—'Command Function Co-operation with Joint Civil Authority.' Something like that, but it didn't cover congressmen—excuse *me,* ma'am—*congresspersons.*"

"Hissssssssssss," Jill said. She walked to the window and stood with her back to Hammer, looking out at the newly-leafed trees. The tornado season was coming into full bloom, too. She thoughtfully rubbed the tip of her prominent nose. "We'll have to wait for things to quiet down some. I can crowd some people, I can manipulate others. I *can* talk to the President about it, but *not* until the pressure and attention let up."

"*Wait!*" Hammer shouted. "The tornadoes aren't going to wait! If the President would look ahead to another summer of carnage across the country, *he* wouldn't wait! He could override this 'study commission,' that Thurlow has flimflammed together. Selby has proved what *I* need to know about tornado-killing."

"I'm convinced too, Dan," she said. "There *is* a way to get the President's attention in a hurry, now that enough furor has whipped up to make him aware of Operation Giant-Killer." She paused and turned toward Hammer. "If you're willing to take a chance with the old equipment. I believe it's called insubordination." Jill quizzically cocked her head at him.

Hammer backed away, as though looking for a place to hide. "Oh, no! No, you *don't*. I stuck my neck out for you. I've attracted all kinds of disreputable attention to myself inside the Air Force" Hammer's eyes were wide with caution. "All I have to do now is sit still and be a good boy. They'll fold up Giant-Killer, mothball the 918th equipment, and *study* everything. I'll go off to a nice little wing commander's job and make brigadier. It'll be just like this whole mess never happened."

"But," Jill said hesitantly, "don't they say there's only a fine line between a medal and a court-martial?" It was clear she was on unfamiliar ground, hunting a final, desperate way to save Giant-Killer.

"Yeah," Hammer snarled. "That *thin line* is drawn along the boundaries of stupidity. Thanks, but no thanks. In a word, fuck you.

"I'll go back to work in the real world," he said, "where I don't have lady flying officers ragging on my head. Where I don't get roped into saying stupid things to powerful people I have no business playing games with. Where I don't have lady senators shooting at me. *And,* where one does not find young dinghead engineers from Defense who are slipping out secret reports to someone we can't identify."

Hammer stopped suddenly. "Say," he said in a suddenly sober tone. "That reminds me; have you found out anything about Creaghmiller?"

Jill rolled her eyes toward the ceiling. "Give me strength," she said. "Not yet, Dan. That doesn't make a hell of a lot of difference now, does it?"

"Yeah, yeah," Hammer said sweetly. "I know that, "I don't like loose ends, though. Do you know anything?"

Jill chomped savagely on an ice cube from her drink. "Not a great deal. The trail points to Creaghmiller being a snoop for the Senate Majority Leader. But, the trail gets muddied up with Thurlow, Pogue, and the Secretary of Defense. The Majority Leader used to be Thurlow's law partner in a firm where Pogue's nephew was the senior partner. The Secretary of Defense comes from Pogue's state, and—guess who got him appointed and confirmed in less than three days, by the way—they all do so much sneaking and snooping for each other that it's hard to tell the henchmen from the barons without a score card and a family tree." She whistled noisily. "But, we are making a little progress, Colonel Hammer. I have people working on it. I have people working on it."

"Hmmmmmm," Hammer said thoughtfully. "Well, my checkup on Creaghmiller is still in the works. My ground exec used to work for the Inspector General of the Air Force, and he's a natural ferret. I haven't talked to my own security people much in the last couple of weeks—what with things being—" He wrinkled his nose and made a face.

"—*rather* busy since Selby got blown away." He smiled charmingly, again. "Well, like you say, it's sort of academic, now."

Jill narrowed her eyes and peered at Hammer over the top of the glass she was holding. "Very engaging, Colonel Hammer. Answer me one question, will you?"

"Hnmmm? Oh, sure. What is it?"

"Am I to take it, from this latest string of charming bullshit, that you are planning to throw in the towel on Giant-Killer?"

"Oh," Hammer replied brightly, "*hell*, no. How about a good, saber charge? I thought your insubordination idea was pretty good. If I was a young and foolish lieutenant again, I might risk it. I can see the headlines—'Dashing young officer flies in the face of Air Force brass.' Shortly thereafter, the follow-up story would read, 'Dashing young officer gets shit stomped out of him.' . . . *(She'll be mad as hell, but the smart bitch is probably recording this. She didn't say anything about* her *bugging equipment; only that she kept other people's swept out.)* . . . At my age and grade the commandment is 'Thou shalt not disobey published orders.' You're suggesting a definite *no-no*. Senior officers who disobey orders get RIFed or forced to retire. They spend the balance of their days playing golf with the rest of the old fuds, counting the rivets in their Levi's, and worrying about their teeth. . . . *(It won't wash unless she is by-god surprised—legitimately—and probably furious. I'm going to have to wing it if I decide something* can *be done. I don't want her messing in, anyway.* One *conspirator does not a conspiracy make.)* . . . Anyway, honey, I've got to get back to McConnell. There's nobody watching the store. Vern won't be down for a couple of days. He's doing some plain and fancy job-shopping at NASA, poking around for a new home. So, I want to get back down to Giant-Killer before the snotty little men with the padlocks arrive. Some of my papers aren't in order, and there's some stuff that needs to be burned.''

Jill suddenly looked defeated. Her last chance to strike a blow for tornado-killing set down his empty glass and picked up his attaché case. He retrieved his hat from the coffee table and absently buffed the silver-braid lightning bolts on its visor against his sleeve.

"Listen," Hammer said awkwardly, "next time I get into Washington, this should be simmered down some. Do you think there would be a lot of gossip if we were to have dinner and hit some of the hot spots? We might want to just hide out in a hotel room for a couple of days and forget about everything else."

"Why, Colonel Hammer," she said in mock surprise. "Are you propositioning me?"

"I guess you could call it that."

"Sure," she managed to say. "I think that would be fine."

"Well, okay, then." Hammer felt so solemn and serious that it made him uncomfortable. "Look, Jill, I'm not throwing in the towel. It's just that you're right about waiting for things to quiet down."

She reached around his neck and pulled his head

down toward her face for a sound, businesslike kiss.
"Stay in touch, you old bastard."

"Sure thing," he said. "You take care of yourself."

"Yeah," Jill said.

To the aggravation of everyone in the path of his
sonic boom, Colonel Daniel Hammer broke the
standing record for the Phantom II on the D.C.-
to-Wichita run. There would be orders cut at the
Pentagon and shipped down through channels. That
would take weeks. There would also be traffic in the
form of verbals with hard copies coming over the
T.W.X. Hard to get around, those T.W.X. interim
orders. You can't get away with misunderstanding
the transmission when it's typed out in front of your
face.

Or, can you?

What the hell, thought Hammer. *Maybe we'll just
have to take it in the shorts. I'll have to have a target
in strike range within twenty-four hours to get away
with it. Still, that would be a hell of a temptation.
Grandstand play.* He laughed heartily. *Now,* that's
*what is meant by 'military adventurer,' Thurlow,
you son-of-a-bitch. Hmmmmm. Sure would draw
attention and just might bust something loose . . .*

Chapter 14

It was nearly dark when Hammer taxied his plane onto the maintenance apron at Giant-Killer Command. The curving shapes of the hangars were silhouetted against the evening sky like beached whales wondering how they came to be on alien sand a thousand miles from the sea. The sunset splashed extravagant color on prodigal low-hanging clouds in the western sky. To one side of the burning sunset, a faint corona of city lights showed the location of Wichita.

Lights were on in the buildings. Dan Hammer gave the ground crew chief a hurried "thumbs-up"—nothing wrong with the plane—as he took off on foot, without waiting for a jolly-wagon. As the dusk deepened and the color of the sky sank further

toward indigo, a full moon began to pick out
shadows. It hung brightly in the clear air, a bald eye
watching a tiny figure move quickly across the concrete ramp.

Captain Stanley Lemm was the duty officer. He
had put down his copy of *Leatherneck* to watch a
T.W.X. message rattling in over the teletype. It
was the one which Hammer had been trying to beat
from Washington.

"Hell, Colonel Dan," Lemm said. "How's life
in the big city?"

"Could be better, Stanley. The D.C. Fat Boys'
Club is shutting us down for 'study.' Selby getting
zapped is the excuse, but there's more to it than
that." Hammer stepped quickly into his office and
tossed his case on the desk.

Captain Lemm unleashed a bellowing stream of
obscenity, concluding with ". . . before I've even
had a chance to kill a goddamned twister, and waste
all that training? I WANT TO KILL A GOD-
DAMNED TWISTER!"

Hammer stepped back into the orderly room.
"Well, you just sit tight, son, and you may get a
chance. You ain't got the best manners in the
world, but, next to Selby, you're the best flyer
around here. What's the weather?" Hammer waved
off the question before Lemm could answer. The
teletyper had completed its message and was rap-
ping out the authentication.

" . . . UNTIL FURTHER NOTICE THIS HQ.
DD HQ FOR USAFCONCOM BLLING—
READ BOLLING . . . . AUTH.
1.685.221 . . . . REPLY."

Lemm stepped to the keyboard and flexed his fingers in preparation to send a routine acknowledgement.

"Hold it!" Hammer said sharply. He ripped the printout from the machine and held up his hand. "Shear off for a minute. Let me read this." He patiently read through the interim order which told Giant-Killer to stand down. "*Hah!*" Hammer said triumphantly. "Training flights, maintenance, and exercises still authorized until Unit Orders arrive. Hah! Send back exactly what I dictate."

Stan Lemm wore a "the old man has flipped out" look of concern as he bent over the keyboard to send Colonel Hammer's answer back to Bolling AFB.

DD HQ FOR USAFCONCOM

GIANTKILLER COM . . . 918TH TEST SQUADRON JOX(DOVJ) 76566

MCCONNEL AFB

SUBJ LAST TRAS XXXXXXX SUBJ LAST TRANS TRAFFIC . . . . AUTH 1.685.221

. . . . .YOUR MSG GARBLED BIXXXXLL THIS END. CAN YU POSTPONE PEND MAINT THIS STN DUTY DAY COMM XXXXXXXXXXXXXX AFTER 0900 HOURS DISREGARD. . . . SUB TO OUR 0900 ANDOR ALT TRANSMIT RETRANSMIT OTHER COMMO METHOD . . . . STORM TROUBLE WIRE ALL DAY.

GIANTKILLER COM. . . .MCCONNELL . . . . AUTH 1.685.221.

The machine was silent for a moment, then suddenly erupted again to tell the world "SNXXXXXXBATBART COM COMPUTE YR INFO DATA WORK PUTURE XXXXXX DISREGARD. . . . .BATBART COM COMPUTE YR INFIRE DATA PUTER WORKING . . . . . .WKING. STANDBY BATBART." It was talking to another headquarters.

Hammer shook his head. "No," he said, "the goddam thing is looking too good. It'll show up on the log when they make a commo audit. Stanley, can you jimmy this thing so incoming traffic will printout gibberish?"

"Sure," Lemm replied. "If you bash one of the cams it throws the printout cycle out of phase." He smiled broadly. "You know, Colonel Dan, I've had 'radio malfunction,' too, when they were telling me to do something I didn't want to do for a while."

"So bash one of the damned cams while I read over the weather," Hammer said matter-of-factly.

"If you'll tell me what this is all about? Sir?" He absently fluffed his walrus moustache.

"My solemn oath," Hammer replied.

"That's a deal." Lemm started digging through the desk, looking for a suitable weapon with which to carry out the Colonel's wishes.

There was a front moving southeast and it would get to Omaha well before midnight. It was already raining in Des Moines. The big computer plotted the weather grid for the next twelve hours and spit out a seventy percent probability of tornado development within the kill range of Giant-Killer.

Hammer decided he would have to take Stan

Lemm into his confidence. Lemm was the Duty Officer and would have to deal with messages and phone calls. He returned to the orderly room with an updated weather report and the computer probability analysis on tornado imminence.

Lemm had disrupted the teletype and was replacing the machine's cover. "Sir!" Captain Lemm snapped to attention and saluted with a heavy screwdriver. "We have met the enemy and he is talking funny." He shrugged his shoulders and pointed to the disabled T.W.X.

Colonel Hammer outlined the current shaky status of Operation Giant-Killer, the oblivion in which Thurlow and his faction were trying to bury the program. He explained that official orders— orders that *couldn't* be played around with—would soon freeze the program for "study."

"So," Hammer concluded, "as long as conditions look like we might get a tornado within strike range tonight, I'm gonna stick our necks out just a little.

Hammer had to pause frequently as Lemm unleashed fierce bursts of profanity vile enough to turn any longshoreman's hair snow white.

"If I can pull off a night-time kill without getting myself and another airplane blown away will show that we can kill these things anytime, anywhere. They'll have to realize that Giant-Killer is a strong program. Dammit, the project deserves better than a bunch of goddam civilians picking it apart."

"I'm with you, Colonel Dan. This is something I can get my *teeth* into," Lemm said enthusiastically. "Uh, who's going to fly it?"

"*Me*," Hammer said. "All by myself."

"*Hell-goddam-son-of-a-bitch!*" Lemm erupted. "*I* wanna fly it! I haven't had a shot at one of these goddamned things yet!"

"Shut up," Hammer explained. "You are the Duty Officer from 1600 this afternoon to 1600 tomorrow afternoon. It would look just a little odd to change that now. We can't afford to mess with rosters, assignments, anything we don't *have* to mess with. Besides, mister rompin', stompin', jarhead, I've had a pilot killed in these planes. Don't forget *that*, Mister. I *will not* send up anyone else. They could pluck my chicken for what I'm doing. But, I lose another pilot and they'll bounce my ass right out of the Air Force."

The phone rang. Both men looked at each other. It rang again. Lemm started to reach for it, but Hammer waved him off.

Hammer picked up the receiver as though it were a bomb.

"*Hallo?*" he said in a thick and probably unconvincing accent. "No, disis Olaf, the yanitor. No, Captain Lemm iss down the hall for a minute. No, ay don't know, but ay think he vent to da john. Yah, he asks me to answer da phone if she bane ring. Yah, sure, I tell him you vill call back."

Both officers exhaled noisily when the telephone receiver was safely back on its cradle.

"We've got to move fast. Don't answer that son-of-a-bitch until I'm in the air and you can truthfully say I can't be called back. I want all this to look reasonably straight in terms of time check verifications on all the goddam military logs and records."

"I hate to say it, Colonel Dan," Lemm said,

"but it's going to look like hanky-panky anyway. The Inspector General and those AFOSI guys can *really* audit the old records."

"Yeah," Hammer said reflectively. He stared at the desk top for a moment, then his head snapped up. "Fuck it! It's not like we were stealing whisky from the 'O' Club, Stan. We're in the right. Besides, it's started now. What you see is what you get, Stanley, my boy." Hammer burned the earlier T.W.X. printout as he spoke. "Do we have a plane on the line?"

"Should have," Lemm said. "I'll phone maintenance."

"Good. I'll check Control; see what computer and radio people we have on hand for attack support. When you're not using that phone, keep the fucker off the hook. We have to prevent them from reaching us until I'm on my way to a target. Or, until we abandon the entire absurd scheme. I have a hunch this is my night to get lucky. . . . (*IT IS ABSURD, YOU OLD BASTARD. AND YOU KNOW BETTER. Yes, sir, I do—I know better. THEN WHY ARE YOU DOING IT? I don't know, sir. TO PROVE TO THAT BROAD IN THE SENATE THAT YOU CAN STILL CALL SOME OF YOUR OWN SHOTS? OR IS THIS A LAST, PATHETIC GESTURE BECAUSE THEY'RE ABOLISHING YOUR LITTLE PRIVATE EMPIRE, YOUR COMMAND? Yes, sir; if you say so, sir. YOU WANT TO PROVE TO ALL THE KIDS THAT THE OLD MAN IS A HOT PILOT, TOO? Well, sir, there's the deep-seated desire of every career soldier to stick it to those damned civilians who really run your show without knowing what it's all about. THAT'S A BUNCH OF BULLSHIT! YOU EXPECT ME TO BELIEVE THAT? ANY*

OR ALL OF THE ABOVE? CHOP THAT SHIT OFF, HAMMER!
SPECULATION MAKES YOUR SHOOTING SHAKY. Yes, sir.)
. . . After I've been to Control, Stan, I'm going
over to the shed to see Mendoza. I'm going to depend on you to get the mission laid on. We'll shoot
for a standby briefing in one hour. And—except
between you and me— this is officially a graded
command exercise, called Pandora. *Exercise Pandora.*''

Before Lemm could reply, Hammer was out the
door. Lemm got on the phone, smoothly setting the
pre-mission machinery into motion. This was the
payoff, the reason behind all the seemingly pointless make-work drills and dry runs. There were
reasons—sound and solid reasons—for the apparently picky insistence on small organizational details, the stacking of equipment in a certain way,
the thousand-odd small rituals which make up the
fabric and substance of a military unit. The squadron necessary to keep Jill Flight and Egghead Flight
operational and ready to respond to need—the
people who never left the ground—ran well over
two hundred persons.

The ground crews already knew what was expected, knew their jobs and responsibilities.
Check-lists could be run out on zero notice. When
the order came down to ''Standby for scramble,''
the entire efficient machine swung into gear. Operation Giant-Killer could go from complete shutdown
to planes in the air in less than an hour.

Operation Giant-Killer's Line Chief was Senior
Master Sergeant Hamilton Jacobi Mendoza. Mendoza had a simple philosophy. ''Any pilot gets

greased in the air, the chances are it could have been prevented if some guy on the ground had been more careful. Make sure it ain't *yer* fault!"

Colonel Hammer was not surprised to find that three Giant-Killer planes were fueled, checked out, and ready to be armed and put on the flight line.

Mendoza shook his head. "I appreciate the fact that yer the C.O., Colonel Hammer, but I can't draw no ordnance on no verbal order for *nobody*. I gotta have a 37, signed by yerself or the exec. Y'can't just go to the bomb dump and get a piece o' accountable ordnance like you'd pick up a watermelon from a fruit stand."

"I know that," Hammer said to the balding Line Chief, "but I want to put one plane on standby for a possible mission tonight. The thing is, I don't want to log it on as a kill mission or a scramble for kill."

"I understand, sir," Mendoza replied, "The word's around that they're gonna shut us down, and, believe me, I can see why you want it this way. But, I can't mate no bomb to no plane without no 37."

Hammer reddened around the ears. *Jungle drums*, he thought. *I swear the bastards have jungle drums. If I stub my toe, these damned NCOs know about it before I fall down.*

"Fuck the paperwork, Sergeant Mendoza!" Hammer thundered. "I want a plane armed and on the line in *thirty minutes*! Do you have any God-damned recommendations?"

"Yes, sir," replied Mendoza calmly. "Gimme a 37 with all the function lines 'N/A,' and lay on the ordnance draw as 'purpose: crew practice—graded exercise.' I'll have yer plane out on the line less than a half hour after I draw the bomb—ready to go—and nobody has to stick his neck out.''

Hammer sighed. ''Excellent idea, Chief. I guess I'm drawn a little thin, tonight. I almost lost my temper.''

''All in a day's work, Colonel,'' Mendoza replied cheerfully. He barrelled out the door of his office into the eerily lit hangar. His rumbling bass voice rolled like thunder, reeling off a stream of bellowed orders.

Chapter 15

Fluffy alps were piling up in the northern sky, sparkling in the moonlight. They were moving fast, changing shape and shifting over the horizon in a steady advance. When Dan Hammer had been a young lieutenant, just learning to fly, the aphorism for dirty-weather flying was, "I'm gonna climb those fluffy alps."

Perhaps it was the clear air that moves ahead of a storm front, and perhaps it was the tension stiffening inside Dan Hammer's body and spirit, bringing a heightened awareness and sharpening of the senses. The full moon seemed as close as a streetlight. The few stars visible in the bright sky blazed like polished dagger points under the moon, and the clean light sparkled on the concrete runway that

stretched into the distance. The black shapes of the
buildings were rimmed with intense light which
danced and flickered over them and along the
ground, seeming to light the grass and the trees in
the open spaces from within.

Phosphorescence.

Dancing frost that glittered with its own internal
light.

The temperature was dropping along with the
barometer, and a chill wind was beginning to stir
itself across the airbase.

Forty-five minutes after Dan Hammer had read
the critical T.W.X. printout, prevented Stan Lemm
from sending a normal acknowledgement, and set
the forces in motion to deliberately disobey the *intent*
of the orders from Washington—with a hopefully
high probability of never getting caught at it—a lot
of activity by a lot of people had come together
smoothly and efficiently. Operation Giant-Killer
was *legally* on a practice standby in a command-
initiated graded exercise. *Actually* it was ready for
Dan Hammer to risk his neck, alone, for the Jolly
Old Cause.

Temperatures were dropping all along the
weather front. A well-defined squall line had
formed, moving southeast. At McConnell AFB it
was as cold as a stainless steel toilet seat.

Computer probability for tornado development
was now up to ninety percent. At one hour before
midnight, it paid off.

Colonel Hammer was suited up, ready to go, and
napping on the old leather couch in his office when
Captain Lemm shook him savagely.

"Uh?" Hammer said. He was awake instantly.

"We got one!|" Lemm shouted. "We got one of the bastards in strike range—an *enormous* son-ofabitch!"

Hammer was on his feet. "Get my plane rolled out," he said, "while I wash my face and go to the can."

"Whoopee!" Lemm howled, as he galloped out of Hammer's office. *"Kill that fucker! Who-opeeeee!"*

Less than five minutes later, Dan Hammer emerged from the headquarters building. Helmet under his arm, he stood for a moment in the cold, clear air, and looked toward the moon. An absurd image of a knight in armor, also with his helmet under his arm, answering a dragon alert, flitted across his mind. He looked toward the flight line.

There was no plane on the line.

Dan Hammer gritted his teeth and cursed. The sound was lost under warning klaxon's echoes. He leaped into his jeep and gunned it toward the hangars.

The hangar door was open. The sleek Phantom II was standing just inside —armed, ready, hooked on to the tow-cable of a tractor.

Stan Lemm had just reached the doorway on foot. Hammer could hear the Marine officer's profane shrieks even over the klaxon.

Hammer locked the brakes and slid to a stop to one side of the giant doorway. He jerked the hand-brake to kill the engine.

Craven Creaghmiller was standing up in the tractor, like a suffragette chained to a voting booth.

Stan Lemm was in the process of calling

Creaghmiller an amazing diversity of disgusting things when Colonel Hammer arrived at the knot of men around the tractor.

"What the *hell* is this all about?" Hammer roared.

Everyone fell silent. Hammer moved slowly through the crowd. Giant-Killer used a ready-line inside the hangar, because there was nearly always bad weather on the apron when they had a mission. The planes were towed out to the line. You could not fire up the turbine inside the hangar. It was too dangerous. By taking possession of the tractor, Creaghmiller had effectively stalled the scramble. For a while, at least. It looked as though he had recently arrived. His hair was uncombed and his clothing was rumpled.

"What the *hell* is going on, here?" Hammer said, again.

Lemm fired a short burst of swear-words, with the obvious information tacked on the end; "—just got here, myself."

Sergeant Mendoza cleared his throat loudly and spoke. "The minute I open the hangar door, this *civilian* jumps inside and asks what we're doin' I says 'Ferget it, bud,' an' tell him he's not allowed in here without either Captain Scott or you with him. He asks me again and I tell him, sorta firm-like, to beat it. The next thing I know, he's hollerin' something about orders being violated. He jumps up on the tractor an' turns off the motor. I tell one of my boys to jerk him offa there and throw him out—an' don't be too gentle. But, he grabs up a tommy-bar and swings on my guy. Then, Captain

Lemm arrived, and, from there, sir, you know as much as us.''

"Colonel Hammer!'' Creaghmiller shouted. "You are in direct violation of a Defense Department order to have your command stand down. As soon as I heard, I came here, and found—this.'' He waved a hand to indicate the activity in the hangar.

Hammer was thoroughly enraged. "What's it to you?'' he shouted back.

"As Defense's representative in this headquarters, it's my responsibility to see that order is obeyed!'' Creaghmiller gripped the tommy-bar tightly.

Hammer shouted back at him. "Stick it!'' He was trying to lure Creaghmiller down from the tractor.

"Does he *have* any command authority?'' whispered Mendoza.

"Hell no,'' Hammer replied under his breath.

Hammer turned back toward Creaghmiller. "If you know so damned much, Creaghmiller you'd know— . . . *(Why, that son-of-a-bitch! He almost trapped me into admitting that I know the details of that order we 'did not copy.' He's not just a neurotic, nutty twit of an engineer. He is working for someone, and he is up to something.)* . . . —you're off your rocker. You're interfering with an exercise. Get down off that damned tractor, or I'll have you arrested!''

"Not so fast, big-boss Colonel Hammer!'' Creaghmiller shouted. "I think you're going to try a tornado-kill. One just developed up in Iowa.''

"*Get off that damned tractor!*" Hammer bellowed.

Creaghmiller laughed. The hair on Dan Hammer's neck prickled. "I'm giving *you* an order," Creaghmiller shouted, "Colonel Hammer! This flight is not going to go up!"

"I'd make *him* go up," growled Mendoza, "if I had a weapon with me."

Hammer scowled. Standard Procedure directed that each flying officer was required to carry an issue sidearm on all flights. He had relaxed that rule for Operation Giant-Killer. Giant-Killer was not a heavy security operation. With all the civilians, congressmen, and the like running in and out, why unnerve them by showing firearms? If he hadn't come to that decision, Dan Hammer would now be wearing a .38 revolver in a shoulder holster. His own pistol was five hundred meters away, in his desk drawer.

He cursed.

But the Duty Officer *was* required to be armed. Hammer edged over to Stan Lemm. "Your gun loaded?" he whispered.

Lemm was carrying his personal sidearm—an issue .45 automatic with the eagle, globe, and anchor of the USMC chased into the handgrips with silver wire, and his name carved directly into the steel on the slide. He was quite proud of it. Said he had spent some money on 'fancywork' for it after each of the two occasions on which he felt it had saved his life.

"Hell, no, it ain't loaded!" The Marine made a nasty face. "The safety officer is afraid somebody will shoot himself in the god-damed foot! The magazine is in the orderly room.''

"I can do that well, myself," Hammer growled. "Why do you jarheads still carry those old cannons, anyway?''

Lemm grimaced. "Fuck you, sir."

Hammer wondered if Creaghmiller was armed. He had come to Giant-Killer in a rush, and he didn't seem to be the kind of person who would likely think of such a thing. "Well," Out loud he said, "I can't let anyone else risk it. Stick close to me, Stan.''

Dan Hammer unsnapped Lemm's holster and drew the automatic, keeping himself between Lemm and Creaghmiller. He held the pistol close to his leg and walked toward the tractor. When he was sure Creaghmiller was watching him, he slowly raised the weapon and snapped the slide back, putting it into battery as though he were chambering a round.

Creaghmiller's eyes widened.

Hammer levelled the pistol, holding it rock-steady with both hands, and crouched slightly. There was absolute silence. When Hammer spoke quietly, his voice carried to every corner of the hangar.

"Creaghmiller," he said, "drop that bar, and get your ass down off that tractor, or I'm going to give you a stomach-ache you'll never forget."

Creaghmiller stood for several seconds, as though he were rooted to the spot. His mouth worked, but no sounds came from it. His eyes glared at Colonel Hammer.

He dropped the bar. It clanged loudly on the concrete floor, and several of the men jumped at the sudden noise.

He got down from the tractor. As he placed both feet on the floor, and Dan Hammer relaxed a little bit, Creaghmiller suddenly reached inside his coat.

Hammer froze. There was not one single thing he could do except wait. An instant became a slow-motion eternity to Dan Hammer as he watched Creaghmiller's hand go out of sight under the coat, grasp something, and then return to view.

He had a small two-way radio.

Hammer started to say "Get him!" but his tongue stuck to the roof of his mouth.

Stan Lemm was already moving.

Creaghmiller had run up the antenna by the time Stan reached him. He had the switch on and was raising the radio toward his mouth when a hard right cross to the jaw knocked him down.

The radio skipped and skittered across the concrete floor.

Hammer was galloping after the radio as soon as it left Creaghmiller's hand. When he reached it, he turned it over with his foot, reached down with the pistol that was still in his hand, and poked the switch with the weapon's muzzle.

With the radio switch moved from "talk" to "listen," Hammer shouted "*Quiet!*" He listened, on one knee, for a moment. No reply came over the radio. Whoever was on the other end had not heard Creaghmiller's attempt to transmit.

Colonel Hammer scooped up the radio with his free hand and got to his feet. He was shaken and sweating, but the instincts developed from years of training and experience kept him in control of himself and in charge of the situation.

"Sergeant Mendoza! Sound a security general alarm," he said. Phone base security and get me some military cops over here to pick up Creaghmiller."

"Yes, sir!" Mendoza trotted toward his office. The security siren began wailing in chorus with the klaxon.

Stan Lemm had Creaghmiller spread against the tractor and had just finished searching him. "You calling the A.P.'s Colonel Dan?"

"Betcha," Hammer replied. "Pull all Creaghmiller's identification—wallet, project badge, the works. Even the change in his pockets. You keep it, and keep his radio. When the guard commander gets here, have him and Andy Scott escort him to a detention cell and jug him for a security/intruder check. Tell them the guy broke in here. We never saw him before. I want this entire base combed for unauthorized personnel. I want it combed *very thoroughly*. Him," He jerked a thumb at Creaghmiller, "I want put on ice."

"Colonel Dan," Lemm interrupted, "are you still going to take the flight?"

"You bet I am!" Hammer responded instantly. "I told you I'm not going to order any of you people up in one of these crates. I've got to do it myself."

"But what about him?"

"He'll keep. Put him over a slow fire and baste him every fifteen minutes till I get back."

"Hammer!" Creaghmiller bawled. "This is the end of you! I'll have you *busted* for this! *Hammer!*"

Dan Hammer grabbed Creaghmiller by the collar. "You'll shut the hell up! You're the luckiest son-of-a-bitch in the world that I'm letting you *live!* If it wasn't for finding out who you're *really* working for," Hammer lied, "I'd just as soon pump your hide full of bullets and then let the Guard Commander take your carcass to the mortician."

Mendoza trotted back over to them, panting. "Wagon is on the way, Colonel," he gasped. "Are you going to abort the flight?"

"Absolutely not," Hammer replied. "Get the plane on the line, Mendoza. Here." He handed the empty pistol to the sergeant. "While your crew is doing that, you march *Mister* Craven Creaghmiller over to your office and hang onto him. I have to talk to Captain Lemm for a minute. I'll catch the plane on the line with my jeep. I've got to phone Control, too, and get a weather update."

Mendoza hefted the automatic. "Hey, isn't this—?"

"*Shaddup!*" Hammer barked. He winked broadly at Mendoza from behind Creaghmiller. "If Mr. Creaghmiller makes a break for it, you have my full permission to turn him into dog-meat."

"You heard the man," Mendoza said to Creaghmiller. "Move. Get those hands up behind your neck and move it along."

The tractor was moving the Phantom II toward the line.

"What else, Colonel Dan?" Lemm asked.

"Don't let them cart Creaghmiller away without Captain Scott," Hammer said. "He just might sell someone on his story. Like I said, hang on to his identification and his radio. When you're back over to the orderly room, tear into that radio, find out what frequency the crystals are, and monitor the channel. Put it on a sound-actuated tape and record *any* traffic on the channel.

"As soon as Andy Scott gets here, turn over Creaghmiller's stuff to him. Brief him on what went on here, *before* they take Creaghmiller to the pokey. Have Scott go with him and tell him to make sure Creaghmiller talks to *no one*, until we know what's what. Find out if he has anyone else on the base, when did he get here, did anyone else know he was coming, where did he get his information—everything. Scott was running a routine security check on the guy for me, but I don't have a late report from him. See what Andy's turned up on that investigation, then sweat the rest out of Creagh-miller."

A big, ugly monster was ripping up cornfields north of Winterset, Iowa. The weather update and computer projection indicated the twister was big enough to eat Des Moines, unless Dan Hammer could get to it first.

If the tornado continued in its path and maintained its current speed, Hammer could get it, even in the aging Phantom II he was flying, about ten miles outside Des Moines, if nothing went wrong. If something went wrong, it *would* eat Des Moines.

Hammer strained the guts of the plane as far as he

dared. In less than fifteen minutes, the storm front swallowed him up. It put the full moon out like a cheap flashlight dropped in the river.

Five minutes later he had the head of the biggest and blackest twister he had ever seen centered in the reticle of his screen.

Hammer gritted his teeth. *Well? This is what you wanted, isn't it?* His game old F-4J Phantom shuddered over the turbulent clouds at supersonic speed. He felt like he was riding a roller skate down a cobblestone street.

Hammer steadied to attack speed at six hundred knots and began talking to Giant-Killer Control, though the radio transmission was breaking up badly. Radar talked him in until they lost the lock on his position.

He had just inserted the attack data into his on-board computer when his radio gave a nasty little *shplook!* and went dead.

Dan Hammer aligned his heading and airspeed with the CompAn Update verification. He double-checked his altitude as he closed with the target. His finger hovered over the manual override button in case the autopilot didn't respond.

The red-and-green grid light blinked on as he crossed the I.P. Dan Hammer shrugged his shoulders and punched the ATTACK button.

Chapter 16

"The big weather news tonight was the tornado that threatened us here in Des Moines. Just before air-time, that tornado broke up several miles west of the city. We're pleased to tell you that Des Moines residents are no longer in any danger. At air-time, this station had not been able to verify whether the Des Moines tornado was dissipated through any effort of the new Air Force anti-tornado station at Wichita. Normal communications with McConnell Air Force Base, location of the anti-tornado project, seem to be out of service at this time.

"Most of the midwest is experiencing rain squalls and thundershowers, which are expected to continue throughout the night and early morning *hours. The storm will continue southeast, accompanied by scattered light hail as far south as Ottumwa.''*

"Halt!" The sergeant swore softly. "Halt, or we'll shoot!" he shouted at the top of his voice.

The running figure did not slacken its pace, though clearly visible in the Security Police jeep's twin spotlight . Heavy rain spotted the shaft of light with reflections and weird shadows.

"He ain't gonna stop, Sarge," the airman in the jeep's passenger seat said. His name was Charles LaGrasa.

The running man's momentum carried him nearly halfway up the embankment before he slipped back. He began toiling back up the slope.

At the top of the slope was an eight-foot chain-link fence, marking the boundary of the airbase.

"If he's gonna try for the fence, why don't he take a chance at someplace else, down the line? That's a hell of a place to try going over." The airman named LaGrasa was fussing with the rain-cover on his automatic rifle.

"You're right," the sergeant grumbled. "He figures it's now or never, I guess. The other squad is working back this way along the fence. He can probably see their lights from where he is." The sergeant's name was Reed Tackett and he was an E-6.

Another jeep slid to a stop alongside the first, slewing around in the muddy grass and almost colliding with it. A voice called out from behind the flare of headlights. "Who's that? That you, Reed?"

"Yeah," Tackett grumbled, "It's me. You got a bullhorn, with you? Mine got wet, or something. I get a jolt every time I try to use it."

"Sure," the other sergeant said. The man with him was tinkering with the spotlights, throwing two more beams onto the bank where the figure was making a third try for the fenceline.

"Well, give him another shout to give up," Tackett said.

"He ain't gonna stop, Sarge," LaGrasa repeated.

"Shut up," Tackett said. "We'll wait for the other squad to come up and then we'll take him in." He turned toward the other jeep, which was nearly invisible in the rain and the flare from its lights. "Go on, Roy—tell him."

The other sergeant was standing in the jeep, shielding his portable bullhorn from the rain with his arm.

"What if he starts up the fence?" LaGrasa asked.

"We'll have to shoot him," Tackett grumbled. "Shut up."

"*You at the fence!*" boomed the bullhorn. "*Halt. This is Air Police, base security. Stop where you are and raise your hands over your head. Stop, now, or we will shoot.*"

The man on the embankment reached the top and paused for a moment to grasp the chain-link fence.

"Y'see?" LaGrasa said.

"Draw down on him, Charley," Sergeant Tackett said. "If he starts to climb, wing him."

La Grasa was already out of the jeep, and steadying his rifle on the top of the windshield.

The man at the fence looked back over his shoulder, into the glaring lights, crouched down, and jumped about two feet off the ground, grabbing at the fence above his head. He missed. As his feet touched ground, there was a sharp, flat *crack* from LaGrasa's rifle. The man's left leg crumpled under him. He would have fallen, but he grabbed the fence, springboarding with his good leg and holding the wire with both hands. He was drawing up the good leg to springboard again.

"God damn it," Tackett grumbled.

The second shot from the rifle sprang the man free of the fence. His arms extended suddenly and he seemed to leap backwards like a diver doing a half-gainer. He hit the embankment about halfway down and rolled to the bottom. He struggled to one knee and looked into the lights for a second, seeming to gather himself for another try at the fence, which was now several meters away. Then he pitched forward into the mud and lay still.

LaGrasa jumped back into the jeep and quickly slithered the rain cover back onto his rifle. "Let's go," he said.

"I think you killed him, Charley," Tackett said. "God damn it. I told you to wing him."

LaGrasa shrugged. "I didn't have enough time. One more shinny like that and he would have been at the top. The order said don't let him escape the base if you find him."

"Yeah," Tackett grumbled. He was putting the jeep in gear. "Call the Lieutenant," he shouted at the other sergeant in the other jeep," and get the ambulance over here."

"I wonder why he didn't stop," LaGrasa said.

"He should've stopped," Tackett agreed. "Fucker didn't have a chance. He should've known that."

"He musta been up to something," LaGrasa said.

Dan Hammer felt his controls *ooze* a little as the Phantom II pulled up into a steep Immelman for the clear sky above the storm. *Damn! Damn-damn! Damn-damn-damn!*, he thought as he felt the response of the aircraft go a little muddy. *Something's starting to give.*

He didn't dare slack off on the angle of his climb until he was sure he was above the tornado structure, and he couldn't be certain of that until he was above the storm.

The plane jerked convulsively as the shock-wave reached it. It was only a jostle, but to Dan Hammer it felt as though something had slammed him into a wall.

Well, the bomb went off, he thought. *That's something.*

Then he broke out of the cloud cover into the light of the full moon. It was almost blinding after the black swill he had been flying through.

As he rolled his Phantom II out of the climb and levelled off, Dan Hammer weighed the advisability of easing back down into the weather to see if he had killed the tornado.

Hell with it, he thought. *Only had one shot at it. Better pussyfoot it until I know what's wrong with the buggy.*

He set a course that would take him back to
McConnell and fell to tinkering with his defunct
radio. Hammer couldn't get so much as a burst of
static from it on any frequency. He didn't want to
put out a distress call and attract any attention to
himself, so he re-set to the Giant-Killer frequency.

"Giant-Killer net. This is Giant-Killer Six talking. My radio is out. I don't know if I'm transmit-
ting or not. I'm coming home. Leave the barn door
open."

He slapped the radio switch to "off" with a savage gesture of dismissal. Then, more thoughtfully,
he turned it back on, even though it still made no
sound.

Dan Hammer began to feel a little nauseous and
his knees were rubbery. He noticed the fact with
some satisfaction. It meant that he still had his
touch. The enormous concentration and pressure of a
strike—flying the mission, delivering the goods,
and then staying alive—had always left him shaky
in the pilot's chair. After the job was done, then
there was no more to it. Just get yourself home alive
with your plane in one piece.

The old Phantom II was shaking noticeably. He
made a series of shallow banking turns which put
direct moonlight on his wing surfaces so he could
inspect them. He couldn't see anything wrong
there. Maybe an elevator was stuck. But the moonlight was too dim for him to be sure. That led him
into a much more unnerving series of speculations.

Hammer quickly decided he had better set her
down at the closest Air Force installation with
enough runway for an F-4J. That would be Offutt

AFB, Nebraska, headquarters base of the Stratic
Air Command.

No radio beacon. No radio means no homing
signal to follow.

Hammer wouldn't let that stop him. He had gotten planes back on the ground that were shot up a
lot worse than this one.

He had never been classified as a possibly hostile
aircraft before, though.

To the watch officer at Offutt, Dan Hammer's
plane was a radar blip which did not respond to
requests for radio authentication. He sent up two
fighters to find out just what it was all about.

Hammer first noticed them as two eerie flames
which showed no lights. Visible to him only by
their jet exhausts, the two night fighters peeled up
from a cloud bank below him. They separated,
coming up slowly on his wings, one to each side
and slightly below him.

One plane would stick with him for a while as the
other moved away for a long look. Then they would
reverse their maneuver.

Hammer knew the two of them were getting increasingly irritated and edgy as the pilots made repeated attempts to establish radio contact but received no response.

*Doing the old aircraft identification ritual, huh,
guys?* Hammer was thinking. *One dog stick close
while other dog pull back and check silhouette. If
idiot try to run, close dog grease idiot with the M61
20mm. Second dog then drop down to deck; make
fix on grease-spot where idiot spread guts on
ground.*

Finally, one of the fighters moved in so tight on his wing that their wing-tips overlapped several feet, with only a foot or so of vertical separation.

That made Dan Hammer very nervous. *Hey!* he thought. *I know you've decided that I'm going to maintain speed, you fucker, but I don't exactly have hair-trigger control of this thing. One stiff updraft and we both get blown away.*

Hammer could see the other pilot's face clearly in the instrument lights. It had a curious and frighteningly alien appearance. Hammer's instincts were screaming in his ear: *Enemy! Enemy! Peel off and dive!*

Reason prevailed. He was flying a disabled F4-J Phantom II. These two guys were decked out in F-15 Eagle fighters. They could grab his old Phantom and shake it to death like a dog killing a rat.

Hammer knew what their orders were. ''Bring him in and land him. Then lead his plane to the security area. If he makes a hostile or evasive maneuver in the process—kill.''

As the two fighter planes expertly herded him down onto the runway, Hammer was thinking, *Hey, guys, it's all right. I'm one of ours. Just don't get jumpy, now. Yes, sir.*

The two F-15s carefully shepherded him down to the security impound area. One plane was always well to one side and slightly to his rear, while the other plane stayed to his rear and slightly to the other side, out of sight.

Hammer was beginning to chuckle. He was tired and understandably tense. He couldn't quite tell if the situation was genuinely funny or if he was com-

ing a little unstuck. *Yes, sir. Don't get nervous, sir.*
There isn't a hostile bone in my body, sir.

Dan Hammer knew perfectly well why the second plane was staying to his rear. Even on the
ground, should he make a hostile movement, the
guy behind him would open up with that 20mm
aerial cannon and just blow the living guts out of his
old Phantom—and probably him with it.

Air Force Security was constantly attempting to
penetrate SAC bases and missile installations. They
would send in guys posing as civilian phone re-
pairmen, for instance, who had something very
minor wrong with their identification. If post security passed them, they would frolic gleefully
around the post "checking phone lines." In the
process, they would place cardboard boxes in
high-security areas such as missile silos, parked aircraft, and the computer complex. Shortly after their
departure, the post commandant would get a phone
call telling him where the boxes were. In each would
be a block of wood, painted red, with "bomb"
neatly stenciled on it. Well, general, your security
procedures get a *flunk* grade this semester. Soon you
may be in a less critical job.

Getting an unidentified aircraft on the ground
was among the spooks' toughest stunts. If base personnel followed the careful procedures laid down
for handling such a situation to the letter, they
passed. And they wanted to pass. Any command
officer would rather risk blowing away a security
inspector than fail such a test.

Dan Hammer sat patiently in the cockpit of his
Phantom II. At the signal, he slowly raised his

canopy and his hands over his head—in that order.
As the ground crew hooked a workstand onto his
plane an officer with a drawn revolver scampered
up the ladder to ask him just what the hell he
thought he was doing.

Hammer smiled when he saw that the officer was
a major. This incident *would* draw out the Provost,
the top-ranking security man on the airbase.

"Let's get in out of the weather," he said to the
major. "This rain coming in is gonna *ruin* the
crease in my pants."

Ten minutes later, they were sitting in an office.
Social amenities had been observed. Dan Hammer
had explained his situation, carefully avoiding any
mention of actually killing a tornado, and outlined
the aircraft problems arising from his "practice
exercise."

"Believe me, Major Carranza," Hammer was
saying to the officer of Air Police, "I understand
your problem, but you're not making much effort I
can see to understand mine. I *couldn't* get landing
clearance or authenticate myself, because my
damned radio is *out* — kaput — busted."

"Colonel," Major Carranza said wearily, "You
were just damned lucky we didn't shoot you down.
As you know, Strategic Air is headquartered here at
Offutt, so our security systems are quite a bit
tougher than on a lower echelon base."

"I know that, dammit!" Hammer said exasperatedly. "We *are* on the same side, Major. Try as
best you can not to lose sight of the fact that I *am*
one of your fellow officers."

"Yes, sir," the Major said. "I appreciate the fact that you are upset by this aspect of the matter. Hell — I would be, too, if I were in your shoes. However, my orders are very specific in this area. I have to maintain security custody of you until I can verify your story." He chuckled good-humoredly. "Shit, you wouldn't believe some of the shenanigans the Inspector General's office has tried to pull on me. Once, I had the old boy himself right in that chair, bitching about me detaining him. Turned out to be a look-alike, posing as General Bunker. The old boy himself was tagging behind, grading our performance. I can tell you I was one surprised son-of-a-bitch when the old boy walked in and said 'You did the right thing, Major. This man is an imposter.'

"Now, let's see, here. The next item on the sheet has to do with your reasons for not proceeding to your own station."

"All right, Major," Hammer said. "Let's just try to get along. You know that I'm the C.O. of Operation Giant-Killer at McConnell—"

The Major laughed and shook his head from side to side. "No, Colonel. All I know is that's what your identification *says*. Under these circumstances—"

"All right, then," Hammer said. "You have the numbers from my plane. Soon, now—it had *better* be soon—you'll have verification from your own line crews that I was getting some buffeting and control stiffness—stuck elevator, I think. Thought I'd better have it looked at before I got into trouble. Better lose some time than risk kissing off the airplane. How long will it take you to get an authentication from my own people at McConnell? Come to think of it, why the hell haven't you done it already?"

"Normally, Colonel Hammer," the Major replied smoothly, "we would have phoned McConnell immediately, but the land lines seem to be out, and the weather has temporarily mussed up our radio contact with Wichita."

A hard rain was pounding heavily on the windows of the office where the two men sat. Win, lose, or draw, Dan Hammer was going to be grounded for several hours at Offutt AFB. "I've got to get in touch with my command," Hammer said. "They may think I'm dead if they don't hear from me pretty soon. The air time on one of these things isn't very long, you know. I'd sure as hell hate to have them call a search operation while I'm sitting on my duff in your office."

"Quite so, Colonel. Quite so." Major Carranza replied. "Let me phone the three-shop for some current poop on that."

While the Major was on the phone, Dan Hammer was wondering. Were the phone lines *really* down, or had the Creaghmiller hassle turned into something which had caused base security at McConnell to seal off the installation? There were provisions in the "mobe plan" which dictated cutting off communication with the outside, except over the SAC phones, but — hell — that would take a national emergency. The more Hammer thought about that the less he liked it.

Major Carranza hung up the phone. "Cheer up,

Colonel Hammer. Our maintenance boys have found out where the trouble is. We can't phone McConnell because a cable went down in the Missouri River. The affected trunks will be back in operation in a half hour or so. As soon as I get an authentication on you, I can turn you loose. They'll have your plane in shape to fly by then, I'm sure. You may have to limp back to your base at subsonic speed, though.''

''Beats walking,'' Hammer said, rather glumly. He was trying not to show his irritation. He had gotten over being irritated at the Major. He was *really* irritated at having to set down at Offutt. Now his movements were in Air Force files. They would irrevocably place him in the neighborhood at the time the Des Moines tornado was killed. He would have preferred to be in complete control of how and when the successful mission was divulged.

Chapter 17

Lieutenant Colonel Marvin Price shifted his grip on the sheet, so that he held the corner of it daintily between thumb and forefinger. He sighed loudly, then let it fall back over the dead man's face.

"Roll him back in," he said to the mortician.

"I'm sorry, Colonel Price," Dan Hammer said. "I've never seen him before."

"Call me Marv, if you like," the security chief said.

"I would have been back sooner," Hammer said by way of explanation, "but my radio blew and my plane was damaged, so I decided to set her down at Offutt. Had to cool my heels while your opposite number up there cleared me."

Price chuckled. "Yeah, I know him. Good man,

old Carranza. Shrewd as they come. Hmph. Wish I had him here to help me unravel this one."

"What's so tough about this one?" Hammer asked.

"No identification," Price said flatly. "You know, it's not every day we shoot some guy going over the fence — but, it does happen. Usually, he's just wounded, and we can sweat him out and piece it together. But — the rain and all, tonight . . . Rotten business, anyway. But, this dingie hasn't got any ID on him — *nothing*. We're going to have to slog it out with fingerprints and dental records."

"Got any ideas?" Hammer asked.

The two men were walking back down the corridor toward LTC Price's office.

"We *know* he was up to something — something fairly big."

"How's that?" Hammer asked.

Price spread his hands. "If we bag some guy at the fence like this, he's usually stealing something. An inside man passes him the goods at the fence. And we have people that will take anything— whisky, electronic parts, camera equipment, ordnance pieces; even, bacon bellies and steaks from the mess hall. Last year we got a guy sneaking over the fence to lay a WAF Lieutenant right in her B.O.Q. Good idea, too — his old lady could *never* catch him with her that way."

Hammer chuckled. "What makes this one so different?"

Price shrugged. "Oh, lots of little things, I guess. It doesn't fit together. Like I say, we catch a guy at the fence, he's usually got ID, *and* we don't

have to shoot him. When the AP throws down on
him, the guy does what he's told. He stops. He puts
his hands up. He doesn't try to run. Like I say, we
bring him in and sweat him out until we get the
story.''

''Well,'' Hammer laughed, ''there's always a
chance that this stiff you've got on your hands is
just a nut — or a transient.''

Price nodded. ''Yeah. Could be somebody who
busted out of some civilian jail — or nuthouse. He
could be a hobo who didn't know he was on an
airbase — you know, just climbed a fence and cut
across. That wouldn't explain it, though.''

''How do you mean?'' Hammer asked.

They had arrived at LTC Price's office. Price
stood to one side and waved Hammer to enter. ''Let
me show you something,'' he said.

Price motioned Hammer to a chair, while he
reached in a drawer for a large manila envelope.
Very carefully and slowly, he undid the clasp and
dumped the contents onto the desk. ''This is what
was on the stiff,'' he said. ''Like I say, no ID, but
he *did* have stuff in his pockets: change, cigarettes,
matches, key to a motel room and this.'' Price
handed over a legal-size brown envelope.

It contained several pages of engineering calcula-
tions, and numbered photocopies of folios labelled
F4J Maintenance Repair Log, and *F4J Structural
Deterioration Records*. These were the portions of
inspection and service logs recording evidence of
the structural weaknesses of Giant-Killer's Phantom II airframes caused by repeated overload. Ex-
cessive sag and flexure was present in wings and

control surfaces. In some cases permanent deformation "set" indicated the incidence of near-ultimate
loads built up by severe buffeting and high-gee ma-
neuvers. It was hard data, ominous for flight safety,
finally confirming what Hammer already knew
about the Giant-Killer planes.

Creaghmiller had made detailed, very precise
dimensional measurements of stressed aircraft
parts, combined it with information copied from
official service and maintenance logs, and followed
it up with engineering comparisons of that data with
the load factors designed into the aircraft. All this
was inside the fat brown envelope Creaghmiller had
delivered to the man shot at the fence.

Colonel Price leaned back in his chair. "Colonel
Hammer," he said, "I think we have a lot to talk
about, haven't we?"

Hammer didn't like the implications in the other
officer's tone. But, he couldn't fault Lieutenant
Colonel Price on his deductive reasoning or his objective devotion to his job. Men like Price *had* to be
detached, because it was their job to suspect
everyone. Experience had taught Price — and Carranza, and Andy Scott, and every other man who
has done investigation work — that *everyone* has
something in his background that looks bad, some
guilty secret which he would rather not discuss.

"Jesus Christ, Marv!" Hammer said. "I hope
you don't think — For Christ' sake! I was sitting at
Offutt when you bagged this guy. It was *me* who
called the security alarm."

Price didn't budge. "I don't think anything," he

said. "I just want to hear anything *you* think might be of some help."

"Well," Hammer blustered, "it's not *my* job to know how this guy got his hands on the information."

"Could be," Price said quietly. "But, it *is* your responsibility. You command the only Phantom squadron on this base. The dingie whose handwriting matches the notes on those papers is the same dingie you're holding on the q.t., a Defense Department engineer assigned to *your* project. I know you've got him. We ran a personnel check because of the security alarm." He smiled. "We always like to know where everyone is when one of these things goes off.

"Right now, Colonel Hammer, your job is to answer my questions. If you're straight with me, I'll be straight with you."

"How do you mean?" Hammer asked.

"Come off the bullshit," Price said flatly. "Your ground exec has a civilian dingie on ice right now — the one you won't let talk to me, the one you don't want me to know you're holding. This dingie you've got worked on your project. Do you think there *might* possibly be some connection between him and the guy we greased at the fence?"

"Command responsibility, you say."

"You know it," Price replied quickly. "I'm going to have a review board that would choke a goat about this shooting incident. You think they're going to call the dummy that pulled the trigger on the carpet? No, it's the old Marvin Price who's going to have to take it in the shorts, even though

LaGrasa says he was only trying to wing the guy. And, brother, I can tell you, old Marvin Price is going to have a *complete* investigation under his belt. If I have to, I'll walk through you and a dozen like you to keep from getting my ass ripped about this. So, start talking, sir, and don't leave anything out.''

Dan Hammer puffed out his cheeks and exhaled noisily. He started talking, and he didn't leave anything out. With a man like Price, it was really pointless to try glossing over little points, like dodging T.W.X. orders from Defense. If you left out something that Price already knew—or had deduced—he would worry that you might be leaving out other things, as well. A man like Price had no compunctions about grilling an officer senior to him. Price was like any competent Mess Sergeant; in his own house he had absolute authority, and woe to the dummy who thought otherwise.

Dawn was beginning to brighten the eastern sky as Dan Hammer finished briefing LTC Price on the entire series of events leading to the embarrassing presence of an unidentified corpse in the post morgue.

The two men had become quite good friends in the process.

''I trust, Marv, that you won't bring out any of this that doesn't bear directly on our dead friend,'' Hammer said.

''Not if I'm satisfied that the security leak was plugged when we plugged the guy at the fence,''

Price said. "Otherwise, I'm obliged to keep digging. If you mean, will I get your ass in a sling over the illegal tornado kill just for the fun of it? No, I won't do that."

Price leaned over and shut off the desk lamp. "Well, I think you're in pretty good shape on this thing, Dan. You initiated an investigation as soon as you smelled Creaghmiller for a rat. You fucked up by not telling me, though. I was entitled to know what you were doing, even if I had never needed to get into it. As far as fucking over Defense is concerned, I might have done the same thing in your place."

"The question is" Hammer said, "how much did Creaghmiller *really* know?"

"Like I say, that's the next step," Price said. "You say your ground exec has been sweating him since before midnight?"

"Affirmative."

"Well, let's go step up the pressure on him; see if any of his seams are going to pop."

It had stopped raining. The pavement was still wet outside LTC Price's Provost office. A damp, chilly wind blew across the dawn-lit airbase.

A thousand images of being up and about at dawn on a military post flashed through Hammer's mind. He thought he had never been as tired as he was right now. He recalled telling Chelsey about early-rising. . . . (*I wish I was in bed with her right now. In fact, I'd rather be almost anyplace else doing anything else.*) . . .

"One thing bothers me about this, Marv," he said.

"What's that?" Price asked.

"Why in hell would Creaghmiller and this guy transfer the information *on* McConnell? That doesn't make sense. If Creaghmiller was handing off engineering dope to this guy, wouldn't it be a lot safer to do it on the outside?"

"Sure," Price agreed. "But maybe he thought he was being watched. Maybe your exec left some tracks somewhere when he was investigating Creaghmiller."

Hammer nodded. "So it could have been like the guy who was fucking the WAF on the base."

Price smiled. "Gotcha," he said.

Chapter 18

Craven Creaghmiller's face turned ashen when Lieutenant Colonel Price whipped the sheet back from the corpse's face.

The all-night questioning session had Creaghmiller worn down, but his answers had remained arrogant and non-responsive. He had roundly cursed both Hammer and Price when they came to march him over to the morgue. "You fuckers!" he had shrieked. "You fascist fuckers! I'll see you both in Leavenworth, you fuckers!"

"Endearing little fellow, isn't he?" Hammer said.

LTC Price made a dour face. "Charming—fucking charming," he said. He turned to Andy Scott. "Has he been like this all night?"

Captain Scott picked at the corner of one eye with the tip of his index finger. "He comes and goes, sir. The sight of Colonel Hammer seems to enrage him somehow."

Dan Hammer was beginning to admire Marv Price's style. The way, for instance, that he snapped back the corner of the sheet to get the maximum shock effect from Creaghmiller's recognition of the dead man showed a refined sense of theatrics.

"We also got the brown envelope," Price said matter-of-factly to Creaghmiller. "He still had it on him."

Creaghmiller's eyes were wide with disbelief and shock. "This is monstrous," he said soberly. "What kind of men are you . . . " His words trailed off.

Price shrugged. "He was told to stop. He ran. He was told again, 'Stop or we shoot.' I hardly think you're in a position to make moral judgements, Mr. Creaghmiller. Who was he?"

"I don't know," Creaghmiller said flatly.

"You're lying," Price said. There was a controlled ominousness in his voice that had not been there during his conversation with Hammer. "You're not a man who has the guts or the brains to stand up to interrogation, Mr. Creaghmiller. Do you expect someone to rescue you from us?"

Creaghmiller said nothing, but his expression betrayed him. Price had struck a nerve.

"Well," LTC Price said with the same frightening control, "I'm going to let you in on something, Mr. Creaghmiller. I have been up all night, as have both of these gentlemen. We are very tired. We are especially tired of you and your attitude. Now, I'm going to ask you some questions. But, before I do, I want to explain to you what will happen to you if you do not furnish me with honest answers to those questions."

Price had Creaghmiller's rapt attention, now. "Are you listening carefully?" Price asked him.

Creaghmiller bobbed his head up and down.

"Good." Price continued. "If you do not answer my questions, I am going to take you out to that same spot on the base perimeter"—he waved toward the body to indicate that he meant the place where the unidentified man had been shot—"and I am going to pump you full of bullets, Mr. Creaghmiller. Personally. *I* will pull the trigger. The last thing you'll be aware of is M16 rounds ripping into your flesh. Then, Mr. Creaghmiller, I will return to my quarters and get some of the sleep your little escapade has deprived me of.

"You will not be rescued. You will not be anything. You will be a piece of cold meat on the slab next to *this* piece of cold meat. My report will show that both of you were killed resisting arrest—for failure to respond. And, in a manner of speaking, Mr. Creaghmiller, that will be true." He paused. *Won't it?"* The sudden inflection of his voice fairly crackled off the walls.

Creaghmiller was sweating. Whether LTC Price really meant it or not, Creaghmiller believed and feared him.

There was a long, pungent silence. Creaghmiller was still sweating. Hammer could smell him, a fact that was comforting because it indicated that Captain Andy Scott had succeeded in making him sweat earlier, even if he had not been able to get Creaghmiller to open up.

In the stillness of the chilly room there was the smell of death in the very air one breathed. Colonel Price had chosen his setting well.

Again, Hammer had to admire Colonel Price's style. Even in his own mind, Dan Hammer wasn't completely sure if Price had been bluffing Creaghmiller or not. He didn't want to know.

The efficient interrogation which followed also impressed Hammer. Marv Price was smooth and quick. His instincts seemed infallible. He would cut into a body of information, first loosening the mass with a series of swift generalizations. Then, he would expertly double back into specifics and details, dotting them with careful overlaps which unerringly exposed inconsistencies.

Dan Hammer was awakened early that afternoon by the thrumming of fists on the door to his quarters. He hadn't had *enough* sleep yet, but he had had enough that being awakened did not annoy him to homicidal extremes.

Response to his question: "It's me—Vern. Lemme in."

Hammer got up and ambled to the door in his underwear. "Jesus Christ, Vern," he said as he opened the door. "What's up? Are the British coming?"

"What's the *matter?*" he asked. "I just arrived to find a corpse in the morgue, the base upside down, and no one at your headquarters would tell me a damn' *thing*. Are you all right? What's going on?''

Hammer smiled. ''All that's wrong with me is jet lag. I was up all night. Plug in the coffee pot while I wash my face and go to the can. I'll tell you about it.''

''So,'' Hammer continued as he poured his second cup of coffee, ''I was pretty much right about that Creaghmiller son-of-a-bitch. He was looking out for nobody but himself. He was an aircraft engineer for the Defense Department, all right, but, he was also siphoning out information to several senators—Thurlow among them.''

''But,'' Graham said, ''that's not a breach of security. The people you've mentioned are all cleared to receive that kind of information.''

''*Need to know*,'' Hammer said intensely. ''*They had no need to know*. Oh, sure, we can't put Creaghmiller in jail for publishing spare copies of reports for government officials *prior* to the time they would normally receive them through channels. In the first place, it would be a tough charge to make stick. In the second place, they'd have him popped out before we could pop a champagne cork to celebrate putting the little bastard away.''

''Okay, okay,'' Graham said impatiently. ''Who was the guy they shot at the fence?'' He shuddered convulsively. ''That's spooky.''

''A-ha!'' Hammer held up his index finger triumphantly. ''That's where we may have his ass! *He* was a security investigator for Langwood-Griffin Aircraft Corporation.

"Langwood-Griffin was Creaghmiller's really *big* customer," Hammer said. "He had been accumulating engineering data that would give Langwood-Griffin a big edge in the development of a tornado bomber. He wasn't just selling them casual pieces of information on an individual order basis. Colonel Price feels, from the stuff we got out of Creaghmiller and the material we photographed at his apartment, that we have enough to demonstrate a conspiracy to fix prices and defraud."

Graham was thoughful. "Yes. Yes," he said, "I can see that. Aside from the advantage they would have in the development of a tornado bomber, that kind of dope would be very useful in general aircraft engineering as well. No wonder the guy was so hot to make it over the fence."

"You said a mouthful," Hammer replied.

"Who was the guy, anyway?" Graham asked.

Hammer had to think for a moment. "Aubrey Nelson was his name—not that it's much use to him now."

Graham whistled softly. "I *knew* him. He was an all right kind of guy. I never would have thought he was an industrial spy."

"That's why he was," Hammer said. He set down his coffee cup on the kitchen counter. "Did you know him well enough to identify the carcass?"

"I guess so." Graham was still numbed by the idea that a former colleague of his was an industrial espionage operator, without his ever suspecting it.

"You feel up to going over to Price's office and giving him an identification statement?"

"Sure," Graham said suddenly. "Sure. If it will help, I'll be glad to."

"I'll put on my pants and go with you," Hammer said.

Lieutenant Colonel Price was wearing a gloomy, stiff-upper-lip kind of smile. "I was right, after all," he said.

Hammer was puzzled. "Right about what?"

"They sprung Creaghmiller."

"What?"

"Pay attention, sir," Price said. "About an hour after lunch, two civilians with security credentials from the Department of Defense showed up in my outer office. They had a goddam *writ* signed by a federal judge. I had to immediately release Creaghmiller into their custody. Zap—just like that. And, I'm required to release Aubrey Nelson's remains to the local coroner, *before* any post mortem or forensic work is done on the body."

Hammer shrugged. "That's what you expected, though, isn't it? It's pretty certain now that someone *did* know Creaghmiller was coming here last night. When he didn't check in with them, they knew he was in trouble."

Graham chimed in. "So, Creaghmiller's attempt to abort the mission last night was just to create a diversion."

Hammer apologized and began to introduce LTC Price and Vern Graham.

Price held up his hand, palm out, and waved it slightly. "I know about Dr. Graham," he said, "though we haven't met."

Hammer felt foolish. "Of course," he said. "I should have known you would."

"Well," Price said to Graham, "One can't really tell. It's possible Creaghmiller may have wanted to stop the mission because he felt it was wrong. You have to do some hard thinking there to determine if he really had prior knowledge of Colonel Hammer's intentions, or if he just got lucky and showed up at the right place at the right time to deduce what was happening. Or, that he was seeking to cause a diversion to cover Nelson getting back off the base. He's a goof, but he's the kind of goof who would think of that. What he misjudged, if that's the case, was Colonel Hammer calling a *general* security alert for the entire base. So," Price shrugged his shoulders and spread his hands, "he's a little ignorant of Air Force procedures. That's understandable."

After they had viewed the remains and Vern Graham had made a positive identification, the three of them returned to LTC Price's office.

"How do you assess the situation at this point?" Graham asked

Price leaned back in his chair and stretched. "The only thing you can be sure of," he said, "is deeper involvement than just buying and selling between Creaghmiller and Nelson. It may be as simple as Creaghmiller selling to Nelson, protected by his 'customers' *inside* the government. Or it could be as big as one of those complex fraud-and-skimming operations we occasionally uncover. The situation is too hot for me to handle alone because of the latter extreme possibility. I'll file a report directly with the Air Force Chief of Staff—I can't afford any stops along the chain of command where it would get buried.''

"Why would it get buried?" Graham asked.

Price smiled sourly. "If any high-ranking Air Force officers are involved, they would jump at a chance of downgrading or quashing my information and my suspicions."

"Do you think there are any Air Force people involved?" Graham asked.

Price stretched, again. "Don't know, Doctor, and don't give a damn. I just wouldn't be doing my job if I risked it. No, what I have to say will go straight to the Chief of Staff. I imagine you guys *really* want to know whether there is any way you can gauge what is going on. Am I right?"

Graham looked dumbfounded.

"Pay no attention, Vern," Hammer said. "He does that all the time. How can we tell, Marv?" Hammer knew the answer to the question.

"Well, like I say," Price said, "just measure the shit as it comes down the pipe. If a *lot* of shit comes down, then there's a lot of power pushing it down the chute and spreading it around. If you just get a little smelly gas, then it was a small-time operation." Colonel Price yawned. "Excuse me. I guess I can go get a little rest now."

"Oh, of course," Graham said. He sprang to his feet. "We won't keep you unless Colonel Hammer has some other things to talk about."

Price looked at Dan Hammer questioningly.

"No," Hammer said. "I'm going to sit tight and tough it out." He shook hands with Colonel Price.

"Get some sleep Marv. I caught a few hours, my-self, but I don't exactly feel like a milk-fed quarter-back. Thanks for everything."

"You take care of yourself, Dan," Price said. "Keep an eye out behind you."

When Dan Hammer and Vern Graham returned to Hammer's quarters, Captain Stanley Lemm was waiting for them. He was sitting on the step, and leaning against the wall, dozing lightly.

As they drew within a few steps of him, he said, "Hello, darling," without opening his eyes.

"Were you asleep?" Hammer asked.

"Yep." Lemm got to his feet.

"Light sleeper," Hammer remarked.

"Yep," Lemm said. "All Marines are light sleepers."

"Why is that?" Graham didn't know Lemm well enough to pass up the bait.

"The alternative has an evolutionary effect," Lemm said, stifling a yawn. "It's called death." He waggled a brown envelope toward Hammer. "This came for you, Colonel Dan—*by courier*. I thought you should look at it straight away, instead of putting it into your distribution."

Hammer raised his eyebrows. He took the en-velope carefully, looked at it, and opened it with his index finger. "Pentagon," he said.

The envelope contained a RIF order, dated that day. Dan Hammer's active duty grade had been RIFed back to major, effective date thirty days hence. He was ordered to take thirty days leave at colonel's pay, while remaining assigned to Opera-

tion Giant-Killer. On the effective date of the RIF
he was to report to the Pentagon to pick up his
orders for a new assignment.

CHAPTER 19

" . . . *And, tonight's final story is a follow-up on that Iowa UFO report.*

"Here in San Francisco, we think we have sort of a monopoly on offbeat news stories. But, try this one for size: Residents of West Des Moines, as its name implies, a small town west of Des Moines, Iowa, reported seeing some peculiar things during a fierce storm last night. Some witnesses insist they were drawn out of their homes by a very loud roaring noise, and that the noise stopped suddenly, at the same time they saw an enormous fireball in the stormy sky. Some of the witnesses to the phenomenon describe the burst of light as an explosion. Others insist, however, while a loud roaring noise could be clearly heard until *the time the fireball was*

sighted, there was no noise of an explosion associated with the intense light.

"Local authorities maintain the roaring noise was caused by a tornado in the area, but they are not able to explain the fireball. 'No comment,' says the Chief of Police in West Des Moines.

"The U.S. Air Force has an experimental anti-tornado project under way, operating from McConnell AFB near Wichita, Kansas. They have had some success in dispersing tornadoes with what are described as 'large thermal devices' by Dr. Vernon Graham, the project's chief scientist. Dr. Graham is reported to be currently in Washington and not available for comment. Telephone communications with McConnell AFB were disrupted last night. When they were restored, officials denied that any tornado-killing missions had been launched from that facility. And—you guessed it— 'No comment,' says the Pentagon.

"As your Channel Ninety-Two NewsTeam made further efforts to shed some light on this weird chain of events, we talked to a usually reliable source inside the Strategic Air Command Headquarters at Offutt AFB, near Omaha.

"Shortly after the fireball was sighted near Des Moines, an unidentified flying object showed up on the radar scopes at Offut. The unidentified aircraft landed at that Air Force Base shortly thereafter. The pilot, apparently human just like you or me, was never seen closely by anyone other than security personnel. His arrival was cloaked in the strictest secrecy, as was his departure, less than an hour later.

"Through normal channels, the question was

diplomatically put to the Base Commander at Offutt. After the fireball sighting in Iowa, had any unusual occurrences *taken place at the government installation under his charge?* Now, *if you want to make a wild guess at his answer, go ahead. That's right*—'No comment.'

"This situation brings to mind a simple question which has plagued this reporter in the past about just this sort of official attitude. *If,* as its spokesmen insist, *the Air Force has nothing to hide then* just what is it they are *trying* to hide?

"And now, for news of the national scene . . ."

Jill Kernan picked up the newspaper and read the headline one more time. She had been reading it on an average of once every five minutes for nearly two hours.

AIR FORCE OFFICER GOES BERSERK: TRIES TO BOMB DES MOINES

She threw the paper down angrily. It landed on top of several more scattered on her coffee table, making the newsprint flutter and roiling up a little puff of debris from the ashtray.

"The God-damned fool!" she snapped. She turned imploringly to Senator Jake Tannenbaum. "Confound it, Jake," she said "just what the hell does he think he's proved? And, where are the damned news media getting all these frigging lies? *Forty-eight lousy hours,* and already there are more different stories out on this thing than there are cornfields in Kansas."

"Two questions," replied Tannenbaum quietly,

"require two answers. You know the media stretch a story to make it play. The truth never travels as fast as the original fiction. Something associated with the frictionless acceleration of falsehood, I believe. Now, for the other thing; you know *what* Dan Hammer has proved, Jill. Stop reaching and start thinking. He's proved that successful tornado-killing can be done not only in the attending bad weather, but in bad weather at night, as well. It was an act of considerable courage, Jill."

"All right," she said, "so he's a big *brave* fool. I'll certainly give it to you that he's got plenty of guts. *But*, the damned *publicity!* An official press release would quiet down the mess, but everyone is keeping the lid on till *someone else* makes a move."

"In the meantime," Tannenbaum observed, "your Operation Giant-Killer is looking a little bit like the Air Force's funny farm?"

"Worse than that, Jake. The press is making Giant-Killer into another Watergate comedy of errors. And, why the hell shouldn't they? The bastards will get a lot of mileage out of it. It's a proven format. And, this god-damned TV news commentator in Los Angeles—he's turning it into a slapstick revue;" She picked up an open news magazine from the coffee table and quoted. " 'The Jill, Vern, and Danny Show is a bright new situation comedy that bids fair to reap good ratings this summer.' "

"Well, Jill," Tannenbaum said, "stop and think a minute. If the lid is on, officially, where could the leaks be coming from? The media are getting just enough information to get silly with. They must be getting it *somewhere*."

Jill Kernan had been pacing back and forth across her office. She stopped, stock-still. "*Thurlow!*" she shouted. "Of course! Why didn't I see it before? That son-of-a-bitch Thurlow! He's leaking just enough of the nutty stuff to keep it alive. Long enough to discredit Vern! Long enough to ruin Hammer's career! Long enough to make *me* a laughingstock in the Senate. It's *me* he's after! Always has been!"

Jake Tannenbaum nodded. "I'd say that's about right, but you don't need to get paranoid about it. I—"

Jill slammed her fist down on top of her desk. "He *welched* on me! We agreed privately to both keep quiet—no public statements about Giant-Killer if he would vote for the experimental program." She waved her hand. "I know. I know. An untraceable rumor isn't a public statement." She inspected the bruise beginning to show on the heel of her hand where she had slammed the desk. "He hasn't *really* broken his word, has he? He's just tried to murder Giant-Killer is all. He can pick up the pieces later, when it suits his purposes, *And*, he can prevent us from getting any political mileage out of it for the party. Well, he can *try*, blast his guts, but so *help* me—"

Jake Tannenbaum nodded. "So you're finally ready to take your turn in the barrel, huh?"

Jill stopped speaking suddenly and squinted at him. "I don't get you, Jake."

"Well, Jill," he replied, "you've had other

people out in front on this thing for quite a while, now. Let me just outline what's been on my mind since I read these cheap headlines. Now, stop and think. Consider who stands to gain the most, who can get hurt, and how they can get hurt, especially if . . ."

Around the Capital with Henry L. Smith

. . .

MILITARY LEADERS PLOTTING A COUP? Such things only happen someplace else, you say? Governments that get overthrown by a 'palace revolt' of the colonels or the generals are always in some country you can't quite pronounce, aren't they? Such a thing could never happen in these United States. Or, could it?

Several years ago, author Freeman Trout's very popular novel, *The First Week in June*, had to do with a NASA scientist's discovery of a fantastic plot to subvert the hardware of the space program in an attempt by military leaders to take over the U.S. after a 'launch accident' destroys Washington.

We thought this novel entertaining, but far-fetched. Last week, though, a comic-opera figure visited us claiming to have inside information about a similar, real-life scheme.

Subsequent checking by my staff proved that our informant had, indeed, been associated with the Air Force's Operation Giant-Killer. While Giant-Killer purported to be an anti-tornado project, we were told its *real* purpose was to iron out the details of a plot whereby any major American city could be effectively held hostage by a single aircraft laden with a nuclear device. Giant-Killer possessed enough military planes to paralyze the entire country if turned to that purpose. Defense systems would be neutralized for the coup by . . .''

Major General Joe Stewart rolled up the newspaper and roared.

He smacked the rolled-up newspaper on his desk a couple of times, then viciously pitched it in the waste basket. Of course Stewart's next call was connected with the same story.

"Yes," he said, "this *is* General Stewart. . . . Certainly, Senator. And a good morning to you, as well. . . . Yes, that's correct. Operation Giant-Killer is carried as part of my Systems Command—on paper, you understand. We monitor the program for Defense. . . . No, Colonel Hammer has the actual command authority. . . . No, that's not unusual. A great number of detached or experimental units are carried as detachments of the Systems Command, regardless of their geographical location. We maintain their permanent records, handle the payroll, maintain the budget reimbursments to the host unit—that sort of thing. Senator, If I understand you, you're asking about the method of such attachment for a joint-service program operation, such as Giant-Killer. We generally go by who the C.O. is. In this case, he is an Air Force officer, so we make the attachment to an Air Force Command because the primary mission function of the program is a flying one. If the function were naval in nature, and the C.O. was a Navy man, the unit would have been attached to a Navy Com-

mand. Reason? To facilitate, command and operations. The C.O. can be expected to function more
efficiently in his relationships with higher headquarters if the higher headquarters is of his own
branch. . . . Yeah? . . . Well, Senator, joint-
service operations are a pain in the butt, anyway.
. . . How's that? . . . We *do* it that way because
we have found it *works* better. . . . That's right.
No, I don't mind answering your questions."

Joe Stewart *did* mind answering the Senator's
questions. He didn't hate civilian politicians like
many general officers. What irritated Stewart about
Members of Congress and the people in the Defense
Department was their confounded pedantic attitudes
toward the military. They seemed to be saying "We
are asking you all these damn-fool questions to
show you how we're keeping an eye on you old
war-horses. Besides, your paperclip consumption *is*
up thirty-eight percent from last year."

Joe Stewart clutched the phone more tightly and
jerked his pipe from his mouth at the next question.
"No," he said quite firmly, "I have *no* plans whatever to court-martial Colonel Hammer. . . .
What? . . . No, Colonel Hammer had *absolute
command control* over the military end of Giant-
Killer. . . . What the *hell* do you mean, Senator?
What the *hell* do you mean by '*in on it?*' The only
thing I know about *that* is the shit I've read in the
papers. No! It's a damned lie! . . . You heard
me *good*, Senator.

"Well, Senator, let me tell you something. I'm
not really too interested in how much *you* people
might want a sacrificial lamb in this matter, but you

can bet your plurality you won't get one from *me*. Hell, no, you can't quote me. I consider this to be a private conversation; if it isn't, somebody will swing for it . . . Is that a fact? . . . I *know* what my job is, Senator. I have had conversations with the Chief of Staff. There is a legal team investigating the entire matter, right now. If they come up with anything like that, there will be a formal inquiry. If the inquiry turns up any military crimes—like your damned 'willful disobedience' theory, *then* there will be a court-martial of the parties involved. So far, there's no evidence to support what you suggest . . . You don't say? . . . When, and if, one is convened, *I'll* convene it, Senator—not you. . . . You go right ahead and hold all the committee hearings you can fit into your—busy schedule, Senator. I think I've made myself plain enough. . . . Of course . . . Good day, sir.''

General Stewart gritted his teeth as he hung up the telephone. He punched the intercom line which connected with his aide's office.

''Get hold of Jack Wintrop at the Pentagon,'' he barked. ''I want an appointment with the Secretary . . . No, not that one—*the* Secretary. Yes. As soon as possible. I want to talk to him before I cool off.''

''. . . *Channel Ninety-Two comes in first for you.*

''*Here are more developments on the* UFO *story the Air Force is trying to hush up. The* story *just won't go away. Our reporters have interviewed*

*scores of witnesses to what has become known as
'The Des Moines Incident.' We have also gathered
information from a number of high Air Force
sources.*

"The mysterious aircraft *which landed at Offutt
Air Force Base seems to be part of a diplomatic
mission which is* not of this earth. *Evidence we have
uncovered indicates the pilot was* not human,
*though the details of his origin are still vague.
However, we can say with assurance . . ."*

Colonel Dan Hammer was RIFed back to major
and drew a verbal slap on the wrist. No written
reprimand would go into his service record.

RIF is an acronym for *R*eduction *I*n *F*orces.
They could accurately call it *R*eduction *I*n *P*ersonnel, but "RIP" would be a bit *too* accurate. The
RIF is a simple method of dumping "redundant"
officers from active service without any complicated legal action.

The RIF was very handy when the size of the
active military was being reduced after a major conflict, such as the Korean Affair or the Indo-China
War. It allowed retention of those officers with the
highest fitness and efficiency ratings while
downgrading the "dead wood" that had accumulated, RIF was kept around in peacetime as a fast,
cheap, and unchallengeable method of reducing the
influence of troublemakers.

It worked on Dan Hammer. He retained the rank
of full colonel as an Air Force Reserve Officer, but
his active duty grade was reduced to major. A
troublesome officer—and Dan Hammer had cer-

tainly stirred up trouble—could "have his teeth pulled" when there wasn't enough evidence to convene a court-martial.

While Jill Kernan and Jake Tannenbaum were discussing strategy in Jill's offices, Dan Hammer arrived in Washington. The initial shock and blind rage had worn off. He was frustrated, angry, afraid, and determined to fight the order as best he could.

It wasn't Dan Hammer's nature to sit still and take it when someone was trying to shaft him. He would at least have the satisfaction of finding out where the order originated. Hammer spent the morning peeling off layers of Pentagon red tape like a patient gourmet meticulously reducing an artichoke.

After a ghastly lunch in the cafeteria, he was cooling his heels in the office of the Secretary of Defense, waiting for an interview with the one assistant he knew personally, Jack Wintrop.

A secretary-receptionist approached the couch where Dan Hammer was waiting. She spoke in sepulchral tones. "Colonel Hammer?"

Hammer noticed that she had nice legs, particularly the knees and the well-muscled thighs. *Takes good care of herself*, he thought. "Yes?" he said.

She consulted a slip of paper. "Colonel Daniel W. Hammer, 568-44-9825?" she inquired.

Hammer put a friendly hand on her hip and looked her straight in the eye. "The very same," he said, as soulfully as he could.

She wriggled a little, but made no move to dislodge the friendly hand.

''The Secretary will see you, now,'' she said.

Hammer shook his head. ''No, no, my dear. I am waiting to see Mr. Wintrop.''

She seemed puzzled. ''Yes, sir,'' she said as she shifted her weight from one foot to the other, deftly moving the hip under the friendly hand. ''I have a note here''—She indicated the slip of paper.—''that, if you are in the lobby, the Secretary himself would like very much to talk with you.''

Hammer jerked the hand away. ''The *Secretary of Defense?*''

''The very same,'' she replied. ''Will you follow me, please?''

''*Yeah,*'' Hammer said.

CHAPTER 20

If the Secretary of Defense had been about a foot shorter, he could have been accurately described as "a sticky little man."

However, he was nearly as tall as Dan Hammer. One could say there was an unhealthy, musty edge to his personality. It may have been the job's constant abrasion; he had been in it since the present Administration had come to power. It is not a job to be envied. While the Secretary of Defense wields enormous power, he is also under enormous, man-killing pressure for about eighteen hours a day.

The two men were convivial. They exchanged small talk and pleasantries. They had a drink together. They felt each other out.

They were studiously ignored by a silent figure

sitting off in one corner on a leather couch. The figure was concealed behind a newspaper. Hammer could only see trouser legs and shoes, and an occasional glimpse of a hand turning the newspaper pages. He assumed it was an assistant or perhaps a personal bodyguard.

"Well, Colonel Hammer," the Secretary said, "you've caused me enough trouble already. Now, I guess you're in town to see if you can cause me some more. Eh?"

"I don't believe I understand, Mr. Secretary," Hammer said.

The Secretary smiled a musty smile. "I had lunch with General Stewart today and he was really leaning on me. He's been drawing some fire from the Senate about you. Wanted me to get the congressmen out of his hair. Didn't you tell him about being RIFed back to major?"

"I'm really not following you, sir," Hammer said.

"I *said*, Colonel Hammer, let's not pretend. I'm well aware that you've asked General Stewart to intercede for you. I don't mind saying that I resent your doing it."

"But—"

"The matter of the RIF came up casually. General Stewart was adamant about it. No, actually I should say he was quite angry. And you have the gall to sit there and tell me you knew nothing about it. You *are* a smooth one, Colonel Hammer."

"Mr. Secretary, I'd like to say—" Hammer began again.

"And, *now*, by God, I find you sitting in the lobby

of my offices, waiting to get at my own staff. I've spent more time on *your case* this week than I have doing my *job*. Colonel, you just seem to stick to trouble like a cockleburr to a hound dog. You're a *senior officer*, an 0-6. An 0-6 should be a leader, an example to the people under him—not a guy who's always got his tit in the wringer. These younger officers see a *colonel* sailing straight into the wind, like this, it makes them think anybody can kick over the bucket, ignore the chain of command. Can you imagine what the Armed Forces would come to if everyone thought that way—put himself and his own interests ahead of the service?''

Hammer's ears were burning.

"Well," said the secretary, "what do you say?"

"I *say*," Hammer intoned ominously, "that I have *not* discussed this matter with General Stewart. To the best of my knowledge, General Stewart doesn't even know I'm in Washington."

"I see," the Secretary said measuredly. "Exactly *why* are you in Washington, Colonel?"

"I'm on leave, sir," Hammer said.

"Excellent, Colonel Hammer, that tells me nothing. You have told me *how* you come to be in Washington. I want to know *why* you are in Washington."

"If you must know, Mr. Secretary, I'm trying to find the son-of-a-bitch who had me RIFed!"

Movement from the leather couch caught Dan Hammer's attention. Out of the corner of his eye he could see the newspaper shaking gently.

The Secretary drew himself up. "*I* am the son-of-a-bitch who had you RIFed,'' he said with elegant simplicity. "I wanted to have you court-martialed, but I was persuaded not to.''

Hammer's soul shriveled within him. *Ooops!* he thought. *You have just fucked up, Hammer. Well, try to pull it out of the fire. Be cool.*

"I'm sorry, sir,'' Hammer said. "I meant no disrespect. This entire matter has been quite a severe shock to me.''

"I can imagine." The Secretary seemed to be enjoying Hammer's discomfort immensely.

"May I inquire into the reasons, sir?''

"You may not! I will tell you, though," The Secretary picked up a neatly paper-clipped sheaf of papers from his desk and hefted them. "that we know—from voice print analysis and from the civilian personnel rosters—that there is no *janitor* at McConnell AFB named 'Olaf.' ''

Oooops! Hammer thought.

"We know, from the examination of ordnance records at McConnell AFB, that one of our anti-tornado bombs is missing. We *presume*, of course, that *you* expended it during your''—he made a nasty face.—''*Exercise-Pandora*. That seems to fit with the local reports of a tornado near Des Moines breaking up under somewhat unusual conditions. Other Air Force records place you at nearby Offutt AFB, with a damaged aircraft under you, very soon thereafter.''

The Secretary dropped the sheaf of papers as though it was something nasty. *"There's a hell of a lot of coincidence about all this, Colonel Hammer!''*

Hammer said nothing. He was studying the ice cubes in his empty glass, wishing the Secretary would offer him a refill.

"As nearly as I can tell, Colonel Hammer, you went zooming off into the wild blue yonder, in four million dollars worth of *my* airplane, and killed a tornado *in direct violation of Department of Defense orders to the contrary!*"

"We received no such order, sir," Hammer said quietly. "Not until the following morning, if I recall the commo log correctly."

"That's what we can't prove;" the Secretary said impatiently. "whether you did or you didn't. And, *that's* why you have not been arrested and charged." He sat down in his swivel chair and breathed heavily for a second. "And probably won't be," he finished glumly.

Lions, 2; Christians, 1, Hammer thought. *Our side is rallying. Bring in your best pitcher and try to hold 'em.*

"I'm sorry, sir," Hammer said, "if I have caused any embarrassment to yourself or to the services."

"Christ!" the Secretary moaned. "You're sorry. The news media are going bananas, and there's nothing we can let out. I've got to keep the lid on, for reasons that are none of your business."

"Yes, sir," Hammer said.

"Now, I'm drawing a lot of flak from inside Washington about you. Damn it, Colonel Hammer, you're more trouble than you're worth. You know that?"

"Yes, sir," Hammer said.

"I can't understand it. You have a consistent record as an outstanding officer."

Never been caught bending the rules before, Hammer said to himself.

"I really think a psychiatric examination is the only thing that can be done, here," the Secretary said.

For you, sir, or for me, sir, Hammer thought. He had to choke it back to keep from saying it out loud. He was still forced to cough rather elaborately in order to keep from smiling.

"Colonel Hammer," the Secretary said earnestly, "would you be willing to voluntarily—I mean, the strain of a career can get to *anybody*—would you consent to talk to a psychiatrist?"

"He would not!" There was a loud rustle from the leather couch as Senator Erwin Culpepper Pogue appeared from his newspaper.

"Aft'noon, Colonel Hammer," Senator Pogue rasped. He smiled. "How's things a-goin', young man?"

Hammer took a deep breath. "I have had better days, sir."

Pogue chuckled. "Ah imagine," he said. "Well, into each life a little rain must fall, as they say, but there's no need for a fella to have an umbrella grafted onto his head."

"I wasn't aware that you two gentlemen were already acquainted," the Secretary said sadly.

Pogue chuckled, again. "Hell, Dempsey," he said to the Secretary of Defense, "Colonel Hammer and I are old chums. Ain't we, young fella?"

Hammer could feel the tension flowing out of

himself as Pogue talked. "If you say so, sir, I reckon we are."

Pogue guffawed loudly. *"Reckon!* You hear the man snap out that 'reckon,' just like it was a normal part of his own speech? You have a way of putting people at ease, Colonel Hammer." He turned to the Secretary of Defense. "Now, does that sound like a crazy man talkin', Dempsey? What *is* all this damned talk about psychiatrist, anyway?"

The Secretary looked morose. He rested his chin on his fist. "Some of Colonel Hammer's recent actions seem to be—ah—irrational."

"Well, hell, Dempsey," Pogue said. "We all act a little cracked, sometimes. Like yo'r suggestion, just now. You think the newshawks are clamorin' for pigeons now; just think what they'd do with the notion that the Air Force and the *Defense Department* had put a crazy man in charge of umpty-million dollars worth of the taxpayer's goods?"

The Secretary of Defense said nothing.

"Let's just let this simmer for a while. It ain't gonna get any better flavor with ev'rybody a-stirrin' it."

"I was merely trying, Senator"—*You certainly are,* Hammer thought to himself—"to produce a responsive projection of the Department's position."

"Ah understand yo'r concern," Pogue said. "You're a responsible and intelligent man who takes the trust of his office to his heart and soul. I admire you for that. It's no reason to make a martyr of Colonel Hammer, though."

"That was not my intention," the Secretary of Defense said crisply.

"Ah understand that," Pogue said. "Let me suggest a near term solution, with your permission, of course."

"Please," the Secretary said.

"I don't think it would be wise," Senator Pogue said, slowly and carefully, "to appear to be picking on Colonel Hammer. It *would* be wise to avoid anything permanently damaging to Hammer's career in the way of disciplinary action. This boy has got influential and pow'aful *friends* in Washington."

"Who?" the Secretary jeered.

"Me!" thundered Pogue suddenly.

In their morning meeting, Senators Kernan and Tannenbaum had determined that Jill should begin an aggressive campaign to revitalize Giant-Killer with a press conference.

Dan Hammer talked with the Secretary of Defense and Senator Pogue shortly after lunch.

While tens of thousands of government employees in Washington were on their afternoon coffee break, Jill Kernan received a telephone call from Senator Erwin Culpepper Pogue.

"How y'all?" Senator Pogue drawled good-naturedly. "Ah'm over here, a-settin' in the oval office, jawin' with the President. Now, the President wants to talk to a couple of points about yo'r press appearance. Y'all *are* plannin' a press statement, ain't you?"

"Why, er—that is—*yes*." Jill finally managed to

get out the word. " . . . *(How in hell did he know?
I guess I've still got a couple of things to learn in
this town.)* . . . Yes," she repeated. "Of course,
I'd be pleased to talk to the President about it,
but—"

"Don't you fret none," Senator Pogue interrupted. "Y'all have drawed this down to a head-
to-head billygoat match. What with things bein'
like they are, an' all, th' President feels like maybe
you should back off—"

Jill bristled. "Now, just a minute, Senator
Pogue—"

"Hold on!" Pogue said gruffly. "Let me finish.
If you run out and jump up on a stump, it'll look
like yo'r jumpin' Thurlow and his party. We'd admire t' get control of both houses next year. Th'
President is a little touchy—*as am* I, *Miz
Kernan*—about public fist fights that could be in-
terpreted as partisan"—He pronounced it *'port-ee-
zan'*—"sandbaggin'. Nobody's tryin' to muzzle
you, but y'all accomodate the White House on this
point, and ah reckon there might be somethin' the
White House can do t' accomodate you."

"I see," Jill answered evenly. "What kind of a
deal are you talking, Senator?"

"Wellllll, now, ma'am," Pogue hedged, "Ah'm
not holdin' up the President's hand for him. Ah get
into plenty of mah own trouble just bein' the Senate
minority leader. He wants ya to brief him on some
points about yo'r pet, Giant-Killer."

Me? The President wants me *to brief* him *about
Giant-Killer?* Jill thought. A little man on an ice-
cold bobsled slid down her spine.

Senator Pogue continued, "He's gettin' connected right now." Pogue put his hand over the telephone, loosely enough for Jill to clearly hear him tell the President of the United States, "She's got nothin' t' hide. Otherwise, she'd o' tried to put us off till she got her story together."

Jill squinted against the television lights, trying to divine Sam Thurlow's mental processes. In this environment, his face was a blank mask locked into affable patterns by thirty years in the Senate.

So far, thought Jill, *I sense nothing of a trap or double-cross, except, of course, for the normal rapaciousness of network news commentators.*

Thurlow's answer to the question droned on, punctuated by his hearty belly-rumble chuckles.

Jill had quickly agreed to the President's suggestion. He had thought a flat and public statement by Jill would smack too loudly of a partisan attack on Thurlow and his party. Instead, the President had suggested that Jill and Thurlow air their views on Giant-Killer in television's arena. It was arranged for them to be grilled on a show that specialized in controversial guests.

Jill was unsure of this forum. The President's "suggestion" gave her little choice. The President did not phone people, even Senators, without having given the matter at hand careful consideration.

"And, how do you feel about that, Senator Kernan?" asked Dan Brewster. "Do you agree, or disagree?" Brewster headed up the Washington news bureau for a major network. Jill didn't like his teeth.

"Neither one," Jill said. She smiled her most photogenic politician's smile. "The facts of the statement as Senator Thurlow has presented them simply do not exist. Estimates by the National Oceanic and Atmospheric Administration show, in hard dollars and cents, how much destruction and loss of life Giant-Killer averted. It saves more money than it costs. With proper funding and a comprehensive program, that dollar ratio can be driven even lower."

Brewster smiled. "Perhaps Senator Thurlow was referring to the death of Lieutenant Peter Selby. What does that come to in dollars and cents, Senator?"

Thurlow started to interrupt, but Jill waved him off. "An excellent point, Mr. Brewster. Lieutenant Peter Selby was aware of what Giant-Killer could accomplish. As the most experienced pilot in the project, he knew that his job was dangerous. He weighed these things and decided to do the job. If more members of Congress had possessed the same vision as Peter Selby, he would have been flying adequate equipment, and he might be alive today. I consider, Mr. Brewster, that your attempt to characterize Lieutenant Selby's death in terms of money is, to put it charitably, in very bad taste."

"In that context, Senator Kernan," Brewster said, "how would you characterize Senator Thurlow's insistence on a very inexpensive anti-tornado program? Would you say Senator Thurlow's primary concern was the best interests of the taxpayer, and that he showed a lack of concern for the safety of the flying officers in the program?"

"I would say," Jill replied, rather snappishly,

"that Senator Thurlow's actions as I saw them at that time were short-sighted. I would also say that it takes a great deal of imagination to attempt to lay Lieutenant Selby's death at Senator Thurlow's doorstep."

"Are you then defending Senator Thurlow's policies with regard to the early formation of Giant-Killer?" Brewster asked.

"Certainly not!" Jill said. "I've made myself quite clear on this point in the past, Mr. Brewster. Could we move on to something new?"

"Of course, Senator," Brewster said smoothly.

Another newscaster jumped in quickly with a series of questions. It was established that Senator Thurlow *did* believe Giant-Killer was a valuable program. Representing, as he did, a "Tornado Alley" state, he could hardly take any other public position. His enthusiasm led Jill to believe that heavy pressure to compromise had been brought to bear on him.

Brewster climbed back in the ring for another round. "What was your reaction, Senator Thurlow, when you learned that there might be an—ah—romantic relationship between Senator Kernan and Colonel Daniel Hammer?"

Whew! Jill thought.

Thurlow responded quickly. "I figured it was none of my damned business! You should know, Mr. Brewster, better than most folks, that by the time a person is a Senator, or a full colonel in the Armed Forces, or—" He injected his most charming, folksy chuckle. "—a network news chief, that person is adult enough to separate their private life from their public responsibilities. In that context, I don't see that there is—or should be—any cause-and-effect occurrences worthy of comment.''

That's interesting, Jill thought. *I wonder what they've got on each other, especially since it was Thurlow's office which leaked the lovebird story to begin with.*

"Since it was your resolution which put Operation Giant-Killer in mothballs, Senator, will you vote for its reinstatement if the study commission approves?''

"Of course," Thurlow rumbled. "My position has always been one of approval in terms of the program's goals and its ability to serve the good of the people. Let me make it quite clear—for perhaps the hundredth time—that my only objection to the project was the operation of such a regional program at the federal level. I think the anti-tornado idea visualized by Dr. Graham and put into operation by Colonel Hammer's experimental squadron may prove to be of considerable value. I have been over this ground before; I believe the American public knows how I feel on this point.''

Pogue was right, Jill thought. *Thurlow can't bad-mouth Giant-Killer in a public forum.*

"And what of Colonel Hammer?" Brewster asked Thurlow. "What are your feelings about Colonel Hammer's insubordination case? Do you feel a court-martial would be in order, in view of Colonel Hammer's disobedience of orders?''

Jill started to interrupt, but Thurlow waved her off. "I feel," he said measuredly, "that it is not a senator's official responsibility to *meddle* in the internal affairs of the Air Force. It is my understanding that a minor communications malfunction prevented the anti-tornado station from receiving its orders to stand down until after Colonel Hammer made the flight which saved Des Moines from destruction by a large tornado. He wasn't thinking about taking the easy way out. He saw a job that had to be done. I, personally, have never questioned Colonel Hammer's courage. He is a most able commander. It is my own opinion that there has been a certain amount of overreaction in the last few days. This reflects my personal views about Colonel Hammer and is in no way an official pronouncement of indictment or defense."

Jill felt a sudden, warm glow, and wondered if her ears were turning red. She decided it must be the heat from the studio lights.

Dan Hammer watched the telecast appearance of Jill and Thurlow on *Face The Press* with mixed reactions and a half-smile playing over his face. He had hoped Thurlow would get tarred and feathered. The sight of Thurlow treading water like mad to avoid getting in the soup with his constituents was some consolation. Dan Brewster was doing such a good job of irritating them both that Jill and Thurlow had almost forgotten they were ready to cut each other's throats when the interview started.

"And so," Jill was saying, "Colonel Hammer's bravery focused attention on the most important aspect of our military administration: *Readiness*. Thank God Colonel Hammer's purpose was to save lives. This is how our Armed Forces must serve, rather than as paperwork factories."

Hammer wasn't sure that had been his purpose, but he was enjoying the pure spellbinding rhetoric. Also, he hoped the boost would help get him un-frozen.

Jill and Thurlow finished the discussion with ex-press denials that any White House pressure had been brought to bear on either of them, urging the American people to keep their eye on the doughnut, not the hole.

The President seemed a little reluctant, but he ordered the re-institution of Operation Giant-Killer, taking it back out of mothballs less than a month after it had been put there. He flatly refused to allow any expansion of the program until a final report was in from the study commission, although he privately urged the study commission to move with all deliberate haste.

There was to be a reception and cocktail party at the White House. There were some public pronun-ciamentos to be made. They were going to award a posthumous medal to Selby; there was going to be a Presidential Proclamation naming the Giant-Killer base Anti-Tornado Station Selby in his honor. Now that the fuss about Giant-Killer was beginning to die down a little, it also seemed appropriate to have one of those more-or-less public showings of execu-tive good fellowship among the recent combatants. In this setting everyone could in the cathartic of "But, I wasn't really mad at *you*, *personally*, you understand . . ."

Dan Hammer agonized over the invitation. It was lying on the dresser, alongside the pair of gold major's leaves he would be forced to put on in

another ten days. He wasn't sure he was a big
enough man to accept the RIF, wasn't sure he could
handle being busted two grades. That's what they
did to enlisted men who got into a public brawl—
bust them two grades. *Well*, he thought, *that's
about the size of what you did—bust the bar-girl in
the chops and tear up old papa-san's saloon.*

The only alternative would be to leave the Air
Force. He *knew* he didn't want to do that. He was
bitter; plain-and-simple. He recognized it as that,
and didn't try to justify it in any other terms. He had
been used, taken advantage of, and now that
everyone else's ass was covered, he had been con-
veniently forgotten—an unmourned casualty of a
fire-fight in the corridors of power. Seduced and
abandoned.

Fuck 'em, Hammer thought. *What the hell are
you made of, Hammer? Sugar and spice and everything nice, sir? No, shithead, blood and guts,
brains and bone. If you can't cut it then hang up
that blue suit and check into the Old Fart's Home.
You think you're* married *to those God-damned
eagles? Hammer, you fucking idiot, grit your teeth,
throw out your chest, walk up to the best-looking
broad at this party, smile and give her the
friendliest pat on the bottom you can; You'll feel
better soon.*

Dan Hammer gritted his teeth. Normally he
didn't go in for wearing decorations on his uniform;
today he pinned on every medal, award, citation,
decoration, and ribbon he had, starting with his
wings at the top and working down to his Vietnam
Service Ribbon at the bottom.

When he had finished, he stood back and admired the display. *Looks like you been pissed on by a cow with the pip*, he thought. *By God, it is impressive, isn't it? That's more like it. Now, have a nice double scotch to steady your gun hand while you put on your pants and primp a little. When you're ready to go, put on your best steely-eyed look, part it down the middle, and walk out into that street.*

If Hammer thought his uniform was an impressive display of his own military history, he was simply not prepared for the dazzling magnificence of Stanley Lemm decked out in the full dress blues of the United States Marine Corps.

He encountered Lemm at the reception, planted comfortably near the bar. Hammer smiled, got himself a drink, and sneaked up behind Lemm unobserved. "Pardon me, Mr. Doorman," Hammer said, "Could you call me a taxi?"

Lemm spun on his heel as he inhaled enough air to curse for a full minute. "I thought they sent you to Tierra del Fuego," he said.

"They will, Stanley, they will," Hammer said. He noticed the gold leaf on Lemm's shoulder. Still smiling, he said "Hey, shithead. You put on some major's coat by mistake."

Lemm smiled back. "Your heart pumps piss, sir. The Fairy Godmother finally promoted me."

A sudden wave of sadness swept through Hammer. "I had been planning to give you my old leaves," he said, "but I guess I'm going to need them myself."

"I'm sorry, Dan," Lemm said. "It's like I've

always said. These civilian fuckers don't care.
We're just something the bastards use."

"You guys watch your God-damned language,"
said a voice behind them. It was Major General
Stewart. "You want the President to know you
people use such God-damned bad language? You
trying to run down the reputation of the military
profession?"

Lemm grimaced. He wasn't accustomed to hob-
nobbing with generals. "Sir, we were just talking
about the shitty, uh, raw deal Dan got."

"Don't sweat the small stuff," Stewart said.
"You want some good news, for a change?"

They both nodded.

"I was just chatting with the Chief of Staff." He
indicated a portly four-star general on the far side of
the room. "He's forwarded Lieutenant Colonel
Price's report to the Attorney General's office.
They think there's a good chance they can put this
Creaghmiller guy in jail. There's a federal indictment going down on Langwood-Griffin Aircraft.
Their lawyers may skate them out of being con-
victed, but it's damned sure they won't be doing
any more government contracts. And, I've heard
some unconfirmed noise about the Secretary of Defense resigning—bad health, you know."

"The workings of justice are marvelous to be-
hold," Lemm said, "but how much does it do toward getting a fair shake for Dan Hammer?" He
lowered his voice. *"Not a fuckin' thing!—sir."*

Stewart nodded. "It depends on whose ox is getting gored, Major." He wandered off.

"Two more of these," Lemm said, eyeing his

glass, "and I just may tell the jolly old Chief of Staff what I think."

"Don't make waves, Stanley," Hammer said.

"Fuck him," Lemn intoned. "He's got no drag in the Corps."

They awarded a posthumous Distinguished Flying Cross to Peter Selby. Dan Hammer accepted for him. Then, Hammer accepted the proclamation naming Anti-Tornado Station Selby.

He had written the citation on Selby. He was also aware that Jill Kernan had convinced the President to indulge in the more publicity-oriented naming of A-T Station Selby by executive proclamation.

What no one had told Hammer was that he had been tapped as a part of the ceremony, too. He was right there on the dais when the President opened the next citation and read it to the guests in the large room. The President was almost finished before Hammer realized they were talking about him.

They gave him the Joint Service Commendation Medal for his work in organizing Giant-Killer Command.

Hammer had barely recovered from that surprise when the President's aide gave him another folio, from which he began to read aloud, stumbling a bit over the abbreviations.

His military aide handed the President the presentation case, but the open lid was in the way and Dan Hammer couldn't see what was inside. He desperately wanted to, because he didn't really believe what he thought he had just heard.

The President pinned on one of Hammer's

brigadier's stars as Jill Kernan attached the other one. She was still fussing with it as the President stepped back and shook Hammer's hand.

Daniel W. Hammer—General Daniel W. Hammer—knew it was foolish, but somehow those silver stars, one on each shoulder, by themselves worth about five bucks, made all the hell he had been through seem worth doing all over again.

Jill Kernan stood on tiptoe and whispered in his ear. "You want to borrow my hanky? . . . You've got tears in your eyes, you old bastard." She kissed him on the mouth before leading him down the steps to take his place for the ritual congratulations.

"I wondered who the hell this reception was *for*."

In a far corner of the room a slender old gentleman sat in a leather chair, one of his legs crossed over the other knee. Senator Erwin Culpepper Pogue laughed quietly as he adjusted the volume on his hearing aid.

Brigadier General Daniel Hammer, boss of the Continental Anti-Tornado Command—or C.G., CATCOM, as the sign on his office door said—rumpled his salt-and-pepper hair as he gazed dreamily across his desk at the rear view of the redhead who was inspecting his "war map." On the wall-sized chart of the North American Continent were some two dozen markers, designated by the same device that appeared on the unit patch—a stylized sunburst superimposed on a tornado silhouette. The markers scattered around the edges of Tornado Alley, each with a circle around it that showed its strike radius and overlapped the kill-distance range of at least two other stations.

Jill Kernan, now the Senior Senator from California, had stopped off on her way home for the Christmas Holidays. She turned away from the map and faced Hammer. "Dan," she said, "shouldn't there be at least one station in California? I always feel kind of foolish when I look at this thing and think of the work I put in for a program that has no effect whatever in my home state. It's abnormal for a senator to do something like that, isn't it?"

Hammer chuckled. "I can never tell when you're being Little Miss Do-Gooder or Tough Old Ward-Heeler. It wouldn't do any good, Jill. California doesn't have tornadoes—well, they almost never do. Even the standby aircraft we have at Edwards AFB is never used for anything but pitch-bombing practice."

"That's a very odd comment to be coming from a general," she retorted. "Don't they *have* to give you another star when the number of people in your command exceeds umpty-thousand?"

"No," Hammer replied. "It's all in fitness reports and retention boards. Where I am now, they give me a complete going-over once a year—physical, flying proficiency, records, admin, maintenance, equipment, and you-think-of-it-they-already-have. If I pass on all counts they certify me 'qualified-for-promotion.' The first time I get passed over on one of those, they hand me the fat gold watch and the one-way ticket out to pasture."

"Oh," she said in a very small voice.

"I'm not one of your empire-builders, anyway, Jill. Can't get comfortable flying a desk. Doris Polanski is about ready to take over this chair. She's been an LTC long enough, been commanding a station for almost a year now, and meets the requirements for full colonel. I'm sure she can handle it. I've already endorsed the promotion. I'd like to see her get one star while she still has some of her youthful good looks and vigor left.

"You know, *I'd* like to get out and start a little bush-flying service of my very own. Something to putter with that would keep me out of a damned swivel-chair." He struck the chair arm loudly with his hand.

"So long as the job chafes you, Dan, we need you doing it. It's the officers who start spending more time on the golf course than on the job who ought to be retired. By firm request, if necessary."

"Well," he said, "I've been thinking about getting married again. But, every time that idea gets to preying on my mind, I just want to have another drink and think about it some more. On the other hand, I really enjoy you these days. When this scheme started, every time you opened your mouth I wanted to put my boot in it."

She came over and sat on the corner of his desk.

"Here's some food for thought. Now that Giant-Killer has proved itself in full operation, there are a lot more possibilities. Why, do you know that hailstorms cause *three hundred million dollars'* worth of crop damage annually? Did you know they can be broken up with pinpoint cloud-seeding? Of course, it's fairly dangerous dirty-weather flying, requiring a human judgement to get the job done just right. And, think about forest fires. Why dropping fire retardants is made-to-order work for a good ground support pilot. Did you know they have just as many tornadoes in central Russia as we do in the United States? The situation fairly cries out for an international cooperative program that would utilize what we've already established with this little old operation, here—''

"Hold it!" Dan Hammer leaped to his feet. "You've already *had* your pound of flesh from me!''

"Well," she said petulantly. "I just thought I'd mention it. Did you know that Defense and State have funded a joint study program to look into the possibilities of establishing a world-wide weather control agency?''

"Good for them," Hammer retorted. "I wish them all the good luck in the world, but—''

"But, *hell!*'' She smiled, suddenly and radiantly. "I've already submitted your name to head it up if it's approved.''

General Hammer shook his head. "Listen, Jill. I don't want to hear about it. Why don't the two of us take a little trip down to Bora Bora? I hear tired blood boils in the tropics. We can forget about joint study programs and just lay in the sun.''

"From anyone else," she said, "that would be an indecent proposal.''

"From me it's a proposition," he said.

"I like it," she replied, "handsome old bastard that you are, and I thank you for the compliment. With my flat chest and beak of a nose, I started out as a mediocre sex-object. That's why, early in life, I began to develop other talents. My honorable opponents characterize them as pettifogging humbug and deceitful chicanery. I prefer to call it invention and resourcefulness—valuable in both lawyering and politics.''

Hammer was beginning to feel comfortable, and he suspected it was a fatal mistake. ''My business is in its slack season right now. I've been admiring your trim fuselage and shapely undercarriage, and the tropical invitation is still open. I think you have a better-than-average chance to cure me of getting up at dawn.''

''You mean getting out of bed at dawn,'' she said.

''We'll talk about the first thing that comes up,'' he said.

Jill snickered. ''Bora Bora should be far enough away from the gossip columnists. I guess I'm your girl, General.''

She came around the desk and kissed him.

Giant-Killers don't have to hurry.

A magnificent new illustrated novel by the author of RINGWORLD and co-author of LUCIFER'S HAMMER!

A MAGNIFICENT, PROFUSELY ILLUSTRATED
FANTASY NOVEL BY THE AUTHOR OF RINGWORLD
AND CO-AUTHOR OF LUCIFER'S HAMMER!

LARRY NIVEN FIRST
PUBLICATION
ANYWHERE!

THE MAGIC GOES AWAY

$4.95   *Cover illustration by Boris*

Here is a science-fantasy novel such as only
Larry Niven could create. And to make this
magical tale even more so, it is stunningly and
profusely illustrated with black and white
drawings by Ernesto Maroto in this special
over-sized (6" x 9") edition.

**ACE
SCIENCE
FICTION 360 PARK AVENUE SOUTH • NEW YORK, N.Y. 10010**

*The following pages are just a preview of the
enchantment to be found in THE MAGIC GOES AWAY.*

A thrilling novel of near future catastrophe!

With the excitement of *The Andromeda Strain* and the sophistication of *Lucifer's Hammer*, SKYFALL is a thrilling novel of near future catastrophe—a catastrophe with a chilling ring of authenticity in the wake of this year's nuclear satellite fall in Canada....

SPECIAL:
SKYFALL will feature two striking covers—one depicting a science fiction theme, the other, the "disaster" novel look. They'll both catch your eye so be on the lookout for them!

PROJECT PROMETHEUS WOULD STEAL THE FIRE OF THE SUN—
BUT THE PRICE MIGHT BE TOO TERRIBLE TO CONTEMPLATE.

A NOVEL OF THE NEAR FUTURE BY
HARRY HARRISON
SKYFALL

ACE
SCIENCE
FICTION

$1.95

360 PARK AVENUE SOUTH • NEW YORK, N.Y. 10010

A Science Fiction Western and Motorcycle Quest Epic!

$1.95

A brilliantly
original novel by the
author of the renowned
BERSERKER saga...

$1.75

AZLAROC

*A planet where the passage of time is
actually visible, where shimmering veils
of energy come down at yearly intervals
to seal everything—and everyone
Present at Veilfall.*

106